TANYA E WILLIAMS

THE BOOTLEGGER'S BETRAYAL

A Vintage Vineyard NOVEL

FIRST EDITION

Cover Design by Ana Grigoriu-Voicu

eBook ISBN 978-1-989144-35-0

Paperback ISBN 978-1-989144-34-3

Hardback ISBN 978-1-989144-36-7

Audiobook ISBN 978-1-989144-37-4

For Erin
Whose love of history & fearless dives down research rabbit
holes led to a victorious discovery—a surname spelled just
right, with a tombstone to prove it.
This one's for you!

One

AUGUST 1955
ELKO, NEVADA

MEG

I'M SEVENTY-SIX YEARS OLD AND MY GIVE A DAMN'S busted. I shuffle between the small living room and the even more cramped kitchen, muttering profanities as I move. She'll be here any minute.

My eyes slide to the open front door as I pass it by, its screen latched as good as the sagging doorframe will allow. I wave a dismissive hand in front of my face, trying to swat away the awareness of my displeasure over the day's scheduled events.

The late afternoon heat is suffocating, yet I refuse to remove the sweater that ensures my warmth regardless of how sweltering the day becomes. The lack of a breeze adds to my discontentment while ensuring my sour disposition at what I've set in motion remains firmly in place.

I've waffled over the decision for weeks. On the one hand, I try not to concern myself with what may come when the truth is revealed. On the other, I've fretted more than I care to admit over the true nature of my reasons for sharing the secrets of the past. I could just as easily die in my sleep and no one would be the wiser. I could take all the memories and things left unsaid to the grave with me. But then again, I lived a good life for more years than I lived an immoral one. Surely, that should count for something.

Returning to the kitchen, I smear saltine crackers with a dab of mayonnaise before adding a sliver of Spam. Examining the plate, I push down the urge to crinkle my nose at the display. My Italian ancestors are sure to be rolling over in their graves at my poor attempt at hospitality.

I've never been talented in the kitchen. George always said as much, though he did so in a teasing manner that, without fail, garnered a bemused smile from my lips. We were good together once. Well, at least I thought so.

"George." His name slips past my lips, barely above a whisper. My mouth, wrinkled from years of smoking, purses in response. I suppose I'll have to summon the strength to talk about him as well. The story is not complete without mentioning George Fumagalli's part in all of it.

My eyes flick toward the small sideboard tucked against the far wall beyond the kitchen table. Trapped within its heat-swelled cabinet doors lies the only photographic evidence of our time together. I couldn't bring myself to destroy the album. Then again, I haven't found the courage required to riffle its pages either.

The sharp stab of George's memory mixes with the unease of what I recently decided was the right thing to do. It's enough to make me care little about what Miss Monroe thinks when it comes to my cracker offering. Her questions are sure to be discriminating enough to slice right through me, and for this, I am far from ready.

My breath, ragged and full of rasp, leaks out of me in a defeated sigh, sending the knife clattering to the counter. I must get a grip and steel myself for what is coming. I'll be of little use, and look like a crotchety old woman, if I can't control my emotions.

Placing both hands on the counter's edge, I steady the tremble that shudders through me by focusing my attention on slow, purposeful inhales. It's my fault for having grand notions. Thinking I could rectify the past by speaking with the reporter. Foolish, that's what I've been.

My fate was sealed twenty-nine years ago when the judge handed down my sentence. I've lived with the shame, woven into my fiber like a second skin. But Miss Monroe's telephone call was akin to a chisel striking a large, round boulder, cracking open to the light of day the sliver of hope that has been buried deep within me. I could have hung up on her when she telephoned. That would have put an end to it. Instead, I allowed the past to slip in through the cracks, haunting my dreams while taking up residence in my thoughts throughout the day. All of it weakening my resolve while suggesting the mere hint of an opportunity to tell my side of what happened all those years ago. The possibility of redemption is too alluring, even for an old woman like me, to ignore.

Several weeks later, here I am, cowering like a small child afraid of the dark, and for what? Plopping the plate of saltines onto the small kitchen table, I chide myself for the weak backbone that has found lodgings within my body. I am desperate for a cigarette. Determined not to cave at every whim that crosses my mind, I shove the craving aside. I'll wait until she's gone to enjoy my solitary vice. One cigarette per day, just as I promised myself I would. A surge of defiance rattles up my spine as movement beyond the screen door draws my attention.

"Hello. Mrs. Bruno?"

The timid greeting arrives as an uncertain question. I stop the huff from making itself known as I catch sight of the girl and find she looks no older than a child despite knowing she is twenty-six years old. I inch toward the door, already dreading the next few hours of my existence.

"I'm June Monroe. We spoke on the phone."

"I know who you are, missy." I give her the once over with my most formidable scrutinizing stare. "You think I get a lot of visitors?"

She has the decency to look a touch bashful through the mesh of the screen, and something I recognize as a hint of compassion rises in my chest for the slight thing. "Well, you might as well come in."

Miss Monroe's tug on the screen's door handle does little to wedge it free. I step closer and give it a shove, sending the door flying open.

"Thank you," she says as she catches the rough edge of it with one hand before it slams against the side of the house. Her quick reflexes cause her bag to slip from her shoulder, and I feel as unrefined as I imagine she assumes I am. I wasn't always this way. I chide myself, still unable after all this time to reconcile the person I used to be with the person I became.

The black cat who adopted my home as his own three years ago, slinks past in what I assume is an escape to vacate the warmth of the house and locate a piece of shade in the dusty yard. I give the cat a dismissive roll of my eyes.

Good luck with that.

The girl crosses the threshold with a tentative step,

bringing with her the scent of a scorching desert in need of rain. "And thank you again for speaking with me, Mrs. Bruno. I realize after all these years you may be surprised to know your story interests me, it's just…"

Her words trail off as I turn my back on her and head, at a stilted pace, toward the living room while tuning out her apology-tinged rambling. Two Mrs. Brunos in less than a minute. I shouldn't be the least bit surprised, I suppose. The newspapers never got it right either. Fanciful lies are all they were capable of reporting back in 1926. Heck, they couldn't even spell my name right. The fact that I was Italian American, and was arrested for doing what every other person in the state of Nevada was doing during Prohibition, are likely the only two truths they ever printed.

I switch off the radio that has been playing quietly in the background and take a seat in the room's sole arm chair. Gesturing to the sofa, its cushions well-worn and lumpy from my own sleepless nights, I invite the girl to sit.

"Mrs. Bruno."

I cringe. My eyes move to the only window in the room, the thick curtains drawn half closed in an effort to block out the ever present Nevada sun. I try not to allow them entry, but the unsavory memories from a time when jailers did not know what to call their sole female prisoner in the county jail, so they referred to me as *Mrs.,* rise to the top of my mind, summoning the chill of damp air and the taste of metal spoons in my mouth.

I wrap my sweater tighter around my shoulders despite the trickle of dampness that is gathering at the back of my neck. The day I left the jail is the same day I vowed to never be cold again. I'd prefer to melt from the inside out in the hot August temperatures than allow even the slightest chill to render me panicked.

Miss Monroe is distracted as she digs out a notebook and pencil from her bag. Lifting her head along with the notebook, she asks, "Mrs. Bruno, is it alright if I take notes during our conversation? I would hate to miss an important quote or date because of a poor recollection on my part."

My lips twitch, but I nod once in agreement. "You can call me Meg." My voice is harsher than I intend. Out of sorts with the situation, or perhaps out of practice in trading in civilized conversation.

"Alright Meg. Then, please, call me June." Moving her pencil to hover over the open notebook, June clears her throat and straightens her posture before setting her bright hazel eyes on me.

Two

JUNE

I HOLD THE PENCIL TIGHT WITHIN MY GRIP. I HAVE barely arrived, yet this force of a woman has already unnerved me twice over, and I haven't uttered more than a handful of words. Goodness only knows what kind of icy stare I'll be on the receiving end of once I start asking questions that are sure to pry into her personal affairs. If first impressions carry any weight, I predict ours will be a prickly interaction.

I never would have guessed at her checkered past if I were meeting her under different circumstances. Given her rounded shoulders and plodding stride, I might have assumed she is merely an elderly woman whose physical discomfort, likely acquired with each passing decade, is the cause for her scowl. She could be someone's grandmother, I might have reasoned, had we bumped into one another at the grocery store.

Though she stands a touch over five feet tall now, I can

still make out the shadow of the woman she was before. The solitary grainy black-and-white photograph that accompanied one of the archived newspaper reports showed a lean, dark-haired beauty that surely turned a few heads in her prime. I shift my hips, searching for a more comfortable position on the sofa.

With my pencil, I write the date at the top of my notebook's page. As the pencil scratches against the paper, I consider where to begin. I'm doing my best to maintain an air of professionalism despite the less than cordial greeting I received upon arriving. I came here despite the objections of my father and the less than firm endorsement of my editor. Neither of them see the potential for a story I am certain has more to it than meets the eye. Both men agreed without a doubt that my trip to Elko was sure to be a waste of my time.

That's the double-edged sword of nepotism, I suppose. Having my father's best friend do him a favor by hiring me as a reporter for *The Carson City News* means two of the most important men in my life feel they can gang up on me about my career, my dating life, and well, just about anything they feel falls under their jurisdiction.

Irritation over my father's matchmaking attempts smolders beneath my weary stance on the topic. I've been dodging his insistence that I make time for a new-to-town gentleman for the past three weeks.

My mother tells me they mean well, but her consoling words did little to change my mind. I can't put my finger on the reason, but this story is one I am willing—no, eager—to stick my neck out for. I can't decide if it is my need to escape the romantic pairing thrust upon me, the lure of a Prohibition tale, or the inkling that somewhere, under all the reports on the events that transpired on January 12th, 1926, there is one side of the story that has yet to be heard.

Sneaking a glance across the room at Meg, I get the distinct impression she is a proud woman, despite her brush with the law almost thirty years ago. When her expression borders on smug, the realization bumps up against what I know of the woman's past. I remember the day I came across the headline, "Bootlegger Queen Dethroned." Questions flooded my mind as I sat in the dank, dreary basement room where the newspaper's archives gather dust. With a scented handkerchief clutched in my hand to ward off the acrid smelling dungeon, I read article after article, only returning above ground to the light of day hours later knowing little more about the woman at the center of the flurry of newspaper reports.

I sought out the oldest reporter on staff, but even he couldn't offer me any new information. Tightlipped, is what he called her while regaling the story that shook the small town of Elko during the height of Prohibition. I went home that evening asking myself who this woman was and how did she become known as Elko's queen of bootlegging? I know the basic details about her arrest, trial, and time in the county jail, and yet here she sits, eyeing me with something resembling an arrogant expression pasted on her face.

Giving my head a slight shake, I try to dislodge any premature judgment of Meg and remind myself of my mother's cautionary words when it comes to the perception one may have of another individual.

Two things can be true at the same time.

I feel my brow furrow in protest at the thought. My mother's words often refer to the love she assures me my father has for me. The sentiment tastes bitter though, given that my father's love seems to come into question each time he is placing demands upon my head regarding the man he presumes is the one I should marry. Meg may very well be guilty as charged. However, she could also have reason to be a proud woman and, as a result, is guarded enough to be wary of me.

I lift my head, pencil poised at the ready. Straightening my posture, I force my eyes to meet Meg's. She flinches a fraction before swallowing hard. Perhaps she isn't as arrogant as I first assumed. Maybe she is fighting nervous agitation instead. This will not be as easy as I hoped it would be.

Though, technically, I've scheduled three days for our interview, by the time I arrived in Elko I had convinced myself this afternoon's visit was sure to be all that was needed. I've spent countless hours talking with others about their lives and days gone by. Not once had any of them shied away from a question, and until this moment, I had assumed Meg would be similar in that regard. I hoped she would be eager to tell me her story before sending me on my way to write my front-page masterpiece.

But as our eyes dance around the room, avoiding one another's in the stale heat of an August afternoon, I find my free hand reaching up to caress the smoothness of the pearls resting against my collarbone. My mother gifted the pearls to me on my first day as a journalist. The gift worked as intended, infusing me with a confidence I had no business wearing at the time. But wear them I did, using the pearls as an impenetrable shield of sorts, while I eventually got my footing in my new position. Months and many news reports later, I feel as though I am back at the beginning of my career, facing down a tough story and an even tougher nut to crack in Meg Bruno.

So much for racing back to Carson City, and the premium story my editor promised was coming my way any day now. As the realization in that my current pursuit is going to take longer than an afternoon, I find myself unsure of what I've gotten myself into.

Moisture gathers in Meg's lower lids though I don't know whether it's due to the oppressive heat of her small home or something far more telling. It occurs to me to begin by asking why she agreed to speak with me. She doesn't know me, outside of a handful of phone calls. She wasn't keen when I telephoned the first time. After that, I nibbled around the edges, explaining that I had come across a news story from 1926 and was interested in hearing directly from her. It took the better part of six weeks to gain a semblance of trust and have her agree to speak with me in person. I can't say for certain, but I suspect it was my mention of her possible redemption that ensured our eventual meeting.

I am still early in my career and haven't made a name for myself during my short time as a reporter. Nellie Bly, I am not, though I am desperate to follow in the iconic reporter's footsteps. I feel a calling deep within me to allow those whose voices have been silenced in the past to speak freely and be heard. This is something Meg Bruno does not know about me—my desire to tell stories that have previously been swept under the rug.

My interest in such things began as a pull I felt from the archives room. Though the basement is the least hospitable place in *The Carson City News* building, I find myself drawn there again and again, often catching snippets of unfinished stories along the way. I suspect a desire to have a woman's perspective rise from the ashes spurs some of my interest.

It took less than a week of riffling through old files to

discover the stories that piqued my interest most were those of women who'd sidestepped conformity and went about their lives living by their own set of rules. The women reminded me of how my grandmother used to nudge me boldly, despite my mother's disapproving eye, to go play outside with my cousins, instead of sitting politely on stiff furniture while the adults sipped tea. She used to tell me that if I didn't come back covered in dirt, then I couldn't possibly be done playing yet. The memory makes me chuckle, certain I never arrived home once from a visit to grandma's without dirt marking my afternoon of play.

Stealing another glance in Meg's direction I eye her as she lifts her chin, sitting a little taller in the armchair. I consider filling her in on my plans, letting her know I am on her side here. In the past, she has been ostracized by local reporters, served her sentence, and held her tongue, publicly at least, for almost thirty years. Given the small and worn out living quarters she calls home, I sense life has been anything but easy for her.

Licking my lips, I raise my chin like my grandmother taught me to and meet her square on, knowing the only way to get to the truth of Meg's story is to start at the beginning. I open my mouth, preparing to ask my first question, but hesitate. The room grows quiet between us.

Three

MEG

THE HAIRS ON THE BACK OF MY NECK RISE TO attention as the girl's eagerness to begin fills the space between us. I suspect it is due less to readiness than it is in response to the false veneer I am summoning to protect my fragile heart. A cough squeezes past my chest, urging me forward.

The reality of the options before me makes me feel as if I'm being buried alive in the middle of a desolate Nevada desert. Like in one of those cowboy movies where the hero is trapped in a darkened cave and all he can see through the small spaces between the boulders that block his path to freedom are the tumble weeds rolling with reckless abandon to nowhere in particular.

A small shiver accompanies the thought, begging me to pull my sweater close around my shoulders while I stifle the strangled laugh that is ready to burst forth at the ridiculous notion. Me, a hero in this story. I think not.

Little does Miss Monroe know how keenly responsible I feel when it comes to my role in the events she has come to unearth. Those nuggets of the past are the culmination of years of poor decisions on my part. I may have accepted the punishment years ago and though I was far from innocent of any wrong doing, I've had to live with the fallout all the while second guessing how things actually came down in the end. But, giving voice to those questions that after twenty-nine years continue to pop up like prairie dogs in my periphery when I least expect it. No, I'm not certain I can do that.

I take pity on the girl and the uncomfortable silence between us and stand. My creaky limbs allow me a relatively smooth transition to upright, and I am thankful for it. "Would you care for a refreshment?"

"Oh, no thank you. I'm fine." June's closed lip expression reminds me of my mother's when she was being polite with a neighbor she had little affinity for. Funny how we read between the lines of a person's words by inserting our own assumptions based on what we see written on their faces. I can only imagine what the girl assumes about me.

I sit back down, my knees buckling at the last moment, forcing my body to fall with a light thud into the chair, ensuring any grace I gained in first rising vanishes in an instant. My head shakes in disagreement as embarrassment blooms within me.

No rest for the wicked.

The girl affords me the courtesy of pretending she has not seen my less than graceful collapse into the chair and instead presses forward with her first question.

"Do you mind me asking why you agreed to speak with me?" Her voice is gentle, and I suspect she has taken the approach the same as one does when talking to a startled horse or a frightened child.

"You telephoned me, Miss Monroe."

"June, please. You can call me June." The eraser tip of her pencil rests against her cheek, indenting her youthful skin with its pressure, as she considers her next words. "Yes, well, I was under the assumption you were inclined to speak with me about the events that took place in 1926. Now that I am here, I'm not certain that is the case."

Intimidated by the forthright nature of her assessment, I feel my hackles rise on cue as the words fly past my lips. "Do people usually roll over and tell you the particulars of their life without so much as a how do you do, Miss Monroe?" My tone is clipped, yet despite knowing this, I am unable to reel back the boorish nature of my defensiveness.

A questioning eyebrow lifts a fraction on June's forehead, and I sense I may have misjudged the girl. Perhaps she isn't one to back down at the first sight of a challenge, as I assumed someone of her young age might do.

Not yet ready to abandon my cantankerous standing, I fix a steely gaze on the girl as my mind whirs with the arguments for and against speaking up about the reasons for her visit here today. How can I be expected to discuss such things? My crime is no less a crime, despite the repeal of the Volstead Act. I remain a convicted criminal in the eyes of the law and worse yet, though the courts are satisfied with the time I served for my act of disobedience, I have yet to let myself off the hook for my part in the entire situation. In the end, I was released from prison only to find myself caged behind bars of my own making.

Speaking publicly when it comes to my side of the story edges awfully close to being viewed as a convenient manner in which to release me from my guilt. I have no intention of subverting my involvement in the crime or the guilt that comes with it, but I can't help but fear others may not think it so. Once the words are spoken, I know too well, they cannot be retracted. When those unsuspecting ones learn the truth, it will be too late for me to guarantee how they will interpret any of it. This is a no-win situation, if you ask me. A ragged sigh slumps my shoulders forward, dragging my eyes away from June's.

I once chose to remain silent on the topic. Reporters said what they wanted, often and loudly, and I gave them no argument. Today, I question the rationale I held firm to so long ago. Maybe things would be different if I had spoken up. There's no one left from our little gang of outlaws to protect, not that I should have protected them in the first place. They put me in a pickle of a situation right from the get go. Even after staying silent and disappearing into a joyless, shadow of a life; I cannot set myself free of the tangle of lies. I never realized, until it became too late, what the cost of protecting someone you love truly means.

"Meg." June leans forward, elbows on her knees. "I should apologize. I hadn't realized how difficult this might be for you. If you still wish to speak with me..." Her words trail off as though she might understand, but her face tells me she is keen to get to the bottom of what she has come here to extract from me.

Why does she want to know? Why does any of it matter to her? I conceal the thrumming running rampant through my mind with a tight smile in her direction. Surely, the girl doesn't already know the truth.

My head shakes, not wanting to believe it is possible. No, there is no way for her to have made the connection. I push the thought to the back corner of my mind. Aside from making a name for herself, why on earth did this reporter zero in on my story? Fate, I almost laugh at the irony of it. The responsibility of being the only one left to tell the truth weighs heavily on my heart. Could it be? Has it all come down to destiny in the end?

My thoughts turn to the others, our little gang of Elko misfits who disregarded the Volstead Act and also the local authorities, with gusto. We were an odd bunch, brought together by necessity for some and ambition for others. I realized far too late; it was the ambitious ones I should have watched out for from the start.

I consider the girl. She is the determined sort, telephoning me several weeks in a row until I caved and agreed to this conversation. I narrow my eyes on her, contemplating her motives with suspicious consideration. If ours is, in fact, a meeting of opportunity, then perhaps this is a divine path toward redemption. I am reluctant to believe so, but a whisper from somewhere deep within me urges the idea forward. This could be the moment I've hoped for. The glimmer of a notion that despite being condemned and imprisoned for my past misdeeds, I may be worthy of forgiveness.

The expectant expression on the girl's face spurs me out of my spiraling contemplation, ensuring my guilt over judging her unfairly rises to the top of the emotions running amok within my caged heart. What's that saying about giving others the benefit of the doubt until they've proved you wrong? I feel my brows furrow as shame creeps in at the thought of my unflattering musings. If anyone should know better not to judge a person outright, it is I.

My mind races as I consider an appropriate reply before

gripping the chair's armrests with both hands. "You are right. It is difficult to speak of such things. I'm not sure I can do so, even after all these years."

The taut line of June's lips softens around the edges. "The reason I find myself drawn to your story is because I sense there is more to it than was reported back in 1926. Meg, I—I thought that together we might unravel the past and give you the opportunity to say your piece. I assume you have something to add to the narrative, otherwise you wouldn't have agreed to meet with me in the first place."

I must admit. The girl is good at her job. Coaxing out the details while feigning a genuine interest in another's life. But what if this isn't a ruse simply to get the front-page story she is looking for? What if she is the truest person I've had the chance to meet in far too many years? I feel a rare surge of optimism course through me. Could it be? What if June actually lives up to the girl I secretly hoped she would be?

Clearing my throat to edge out the emotion from my words, I feel I am on the verge of taking a chance. I weigh the cost of speaking up against the fear of remaining misunderstood for eternity.

Strength has little to do with it. I am reminded of the words the jailhouse priest whispered to me in my hour of need. *Being brave and humble goes hand in hand when seeking forgiveness,* he said. *Being vulnerable though, is the only true path toward becoming humble, Mariagrazia.*

With a hasty inhale, I lift my chin and set my determination in place. "I suppose I have two options. I can either go down as an outcast or I can set the story straight once and for all."

Four

JUNE

MEG'S WORDS LIFT MY SPIRITS ALONG WITH MY posture. Thank heavens, now we're getting somewhere. Maybe this won't take three full days after all, and I'll be back in Carson City in no time.

Flipping the pages in my notebook, I am reminded of my bookshelf at home. The one filled with notebooks just like this one. Despite being crammed full and a tad unsightly with its bowing shelves, it is one of my most treasured possessions. To me, it is the promise of my future as a reporter. Representative of my hard work and diligent note taking with pages infused with my passion to tell the heart of a story.

A thrill of excitement rises in me as I locate my previous notes taken from the archived articles prior to contacting Meg. Wanting her to feel comfortable in my company, I decide baring a little of my perspective might help ease Meg's discomfort.

"You should know, I personally, do not believe Prohibition was a productive venture for our country. I understand the original intent was to better a society which had found itself deep in the trenches of a nationwide war against the abuse of alcohol but I do not subscribe to the theory that the only way to fix the situation was an all-out ban of the substance. Of course, hindsight being what it is, I am sure I am not alone in my assessment."

Meg signals her agreement with a bob of her head and I press on, gaining confidence in the strides we are making.

"In my research, I learned that despite the rest of the country going dry, Nevada as a whole didn't seem to put much stock in the Volstead Act. I even came across one article that stated that as little as three percent of the state's population was in favor of Prohibition."

Tucking a rogue strand of hair behind my right ear, I lean in, intent to convey my understanding.

"I want you to know, I am more than aware that if the people of Nevada weren't producing or selling alcohol, they were almost certainly drinking it. Then there is the fact that you were not alone in your actions, Meg. There were seven other individuals arrested that same day. With the sentiment of the time being what it was, I have an inkling that you may have simply found yourself in the crosshairs of an ill-advised law."

Meg's expression remains indifferent as my head dips to read from my notebook. "When I came across your—um— the story headline stating eight hundred and twenty gallons of wine had been seized and destroyed, I have to admit, I had several questions the newspaper articles didn't answer."

"What sort of questions?" Meg's voice is full of rasp, and I choose to believe it is from the warm, dry air instead of bubbling emotion that I might be responsible for bringing about.

"Wine is an interesting choice for a bootlegged substance in Nevada. Given the more than plentiful supply of moonshine and the lack of vineyards in the region, I mean." I lift my eyes and wait for Meg's reaction, but when there is none, I push on. "But we'll get back to that."

I rein in my enthusiasm, not wanting to put the woman off again. "Is it true that Prohibition officers dumped all eight hundred gallons of confiscated wine into the Humboldt River?"

Meg shrugs her shoulders as a small smile lifts the corners of her mouth. "Lucky fish."

The corners of my lips curve upward in response, noting for the first time, Meg has a sense of humor.

Within seconds, her expression returns to one of a subdued nature. "In all honesty, I haven't the foggiest what they did with the wine. I was detained by the time things got as far as that."

"Right. Of course. I'm sorry, I should have realized the timeline of events." Stumbling over my words, I worry my questions are sounding either like something a fourth grader might ask or worse, are close to touching on tender ground.

In an attempt to hide my embarrassment, I allow my eyes to scan the room. I immediately notice the lack of personal effects. The room isn't large, but its drabness makes it feel smaller than it is. Aside from the few pieces of furniture, a handful of outdated magazines, and a scrapbook of sorts resting on the coffee table, there is nothing in this room to indicate the home belongs to this woman. Either Meg is not one for acquiring possessions or she isn't the least bit sentimental.

Coercing my thoughts back to the task at hand, I pick up the conversation where I left it. "I suppose we can take the reporter's word for how the wine was disposed of, given that it was printed."

Meg's head snaps in my direction, her eyes blazing with anger. "That is where you are mistaken, June."

I note the change in Meg's use of my first name and though she seems ready to leap from her chair to contradict my statement, I assume her address of me is a sign that she has taken this step toward familiarity as we attempt to build rapport with one another.

"The reporters who wrote about me did not hold themselves in such regard as to record the truth. You'd have to be a fool to blindly believe anything they published."

"Oh." I have little say in defense of her accusations. Sensing Meg is about to descend into a spiky opponent once more, I do my utmost not to poke about and instead wait for her to enlighten me.

"I have never known a bunch of scoundrels such as those reporters, and you have to admit, given the company I've kept in the past, that is saying something." Meg narrows her gaze pointedly in my direction.

"I'm sure they were only doing what they thought was right—" My words are cut off from under me.

"If you think you can come into my home and tell me you subscribe to the same code of ethics as those thugs, then you've got another think coming, missy."

Meg's words are sharp as daggers and if I weren't aware of my instinctive desire to dodge them, I wouldn't be forcing myself to breathe slow, purposeful breaths while remaining seated in place, doing my best not to appear flustered. During my first week as a reporter, my editor told me about the storms I'd experience if I ever found myself engaged in an interview with someone who wasn't ready to talk. I recognize this in Meg and all I can hope is that her storm will blow itself out before one of its gusts takes me down.

Meg's voice rises another octave and though she remains seated, I can feel the heat of her words from across the room. "Those men filled their newspapers with filth and lies before happily heading home to their wives and children. Do you think they ever gave anyone they vilified by day another thought come dinner time?"

I sit as still as a statue, not daring to utter a word. All I can do is watch and wait for an opportunity where I can show Meg I am different from those men she despises so vehemently.

I hear the crack in her voice before a pained expression stretches across her face.

"Don't you see? Once something is in print, it becomes the only truth anyone who reads it is aware of. It becomes a gospel truth that is then passed on further through time and gossip. That is the power they have and they wield it however they desire."

My bottom lip slips between my teeth as an unsettling awareness slides into my periphery. I am more like those reporters Meg speaks ill of than I realized. Here I am, coming to a stranger and demanding she bare her soul, not for her sake but for mine. So I can prove myself as a journalist—further my career. Shame creeps in like a shadow and my gaze shifts toward the floor in response.

"Even you, all these years later, found their version of my story. It never ends." Resignation takes the place of Meg's anger and, though I wouldn't have believed it could be true, her defeat takes up more space than her anger ever could.

I can't help but empathize with Meg's predicament, but as the room grows silent between us, a new thought occurs to me. "You said that once it is in print, it is gospel."

Lifting her gaze to meet mine, the moisture gathering in Meg's eyes pushes me to take a chance, showing her I can be brave, too, even when things appear unsurmountable. I don't know for sure if anything I write will be successful or even change the minds of how the reading public might view people like Meg, those who found themselves caught up on the illegal side of Prohibition. "Then why don't we make sure the truth—your truth—becomes the only thing people remember about you?"

The woman releases a slow exhale as her chin descends toward her chest. All I can assume is she is considering her options. I hold my tongue and give her the time she needs to recover herself.

Five

MAY 1922

NAPA VALLEY, CALIFORNIA

MEG

THE SPRING SUN WARMS MY BACK, SMOOTHING away the chill of the Napa Valley morning with its gentle rays. The scent of dirt, awakening from beneath its dew-covered blanket, reaches my nose as I disturb its slumber by inching my way along the row of vines.

Tasked this Saturday morning with checking the progress of my family's grape vines, I am bent at the waist, looking up through the greenery when he appears at my side. His tall frame blocks out both light and warmth, eliciting a shiver through my forty-three-year-old spinster form.

"Hey, I've been trying to get you alone for days." My brother, who has been visiting the family vineyard for the past week, interrupts me and my quiet enjoyment of the day.

I toss a questioning expression over my shoulder while taking another step down the row. "You must not have tried too hard then since I've been in among the vines for the past three days. I'm not that difficult to find."

Matteo ignores my slight, choosing instead to press on. "I've got a job for you."

My knee-jerk response is to launch into my sibling, six years my senior, with a litany of arguments to once again assert my position that just because I am an unmarried woman who continues to live under our parents' roof, does not make me someone he can pass his vineyard responsibilities off on. As it is, he only makes the eight-hour drive from Elko, Nevada to the family home twice a year. Once in spring and once during the harvest, never bringing with him his wife and children, despite them being invited on every single occasion.

Though our parents were disheartened by Matteo's desire to leave California altogether, the isolation from their grandchildren has remained a contentious point between them since he first left the vineyard in search of a new life. More than once, I've heard my mother crying in the kitchen after the news that my brother's visit home will be another solo trip to Napa. Several years ago, I suggested they travel to Nevada themselves, but when my father mentioned the idea to Matteo, that too was shut down with a swift hand. The years have lessened the blow, especially since his children are now adults and complete strangers to us, but I suspect my mother's broken heart is unlikely to ever recover from the situation.

I've met my sister-in-law all of two times. Once at the announcement of their engagement and then again, a few months later, at what I imagined was a shotgun wedding. After that, Matteo became even more distant as his life's responsibilities became greater.

My brother has never admitted it is true, but I can't help but feel the scorn toward us has something to do with either

her family not thinking ours is good enough or Matteo's own self-importance getting in the way. Given his desire to become someone of a higher standing than a grape farmer, I assume the latter is a more accurate assessment of the situation. Either way, I force the sensitive topic from my mind whenever he is near and instead choose to slip back into our childhood sibling roles as though I am nine and he fifteen.

Why he bothers to return every year continued to confound me until the day my father let it slip that Matteo was receiving a vineyard stipend. His sole obligation is to return twice a year to help with the spring planning and the fall harvest. For those two weeks my father is afforded the luxury of delighting in his delusion that one day, his son will return to continue what my father started.

Tucking both the inequity of the situation and the divide that has settled between us over the years to the back of my mind, I opt for a less hostile yet still pointed response. "Guess you didn't notice I already have a job."

"No, Maria. This is big."

Matteo's shortened version of my name, Mariagrazia, yanks my head his way, bringing a smile to my lips. Despite our once close connection dwindling through the years, I can't help but relish his attention on me with the secret nickname. He is and always will be my big brother and that has to count for something, I tell myself, eager to have his light shine on me.

Our parents have never afforded us the enjoyment of shortening our Italian names, hence Matteo keeping my nickname solely between us. Determined, they are, to keep our heritage forever in the forefront of our minds regardless of what is preferable among a modern world. I'll never forget how the family farmhouse erupted with a heated argument twenty-seven years ago when my brother announced he was changing his name to Matt Johnson so he could acquire a job as a Nevada policeman.

Sometimes I wonder if our family unit might be a touch more content had my parents acquiesced, allowing him to be his own man. I shake my head at the no-win situation and give him my full attention, since I know that when Matteo calls me Maria, he always has something important to share.

I stand, hands on hips, stretching the kinks out by bending backwards at my waist. "Well, out with it then."

"You know we've secured the permit?" Matteo's eyes light up at the mention of the sacramental wine permit that will allow Brunelli Vineyard to continue producing wine despite the laws that have prohibited alcohol consumption nationwide since 1920.

"And that would be why I am out here, actually tending the vines." I turn my attention back to the row of Zinfandel grapes, but not before issuing my brother an exaggerated eye roll, letting him know, in no uncertain terms, that he is losing his touch.

"Geez. When did you become such a bluenose?" Stepping alongside me, he continues. "Father has decided to expand the vineyard. With the permit and other wineries in the region closing up shop, there is an opportunity to grow as a supplier for the church."

I don't bother to look up. "This is nothing new to me."

Matteo places a hand on my shoulder, coaxing me to meet his eyes. "With the permit, the church is required, by law, to appoint a manager for the vineyard." His smile grows wide, and I recognize the hint of mischievousness within it. "I have struck a deal with the church manager who will be in charge of the sacramental wine from our vineyard."

"Why? I thought everything was settled. We are scheduled to label and ship everything out over the next few weeks. Father has—"

"I thought you were smarter than that." He shoots me a questioning look as he continues to talk over me. "Do you really think the church needs every drop of wine we produce?"

His words push me back on my heels, the weight of understanding making the heels of my boots sink further into the soft ground. The answer is obvious. They wouldn't need our wine or any of our neighbors' wine either. Prohibition certainly didn't alter the quantity of wine required by the Catholic church and since sacramental wine finally got the legal go ahead earlier this year, the increase in demand can only be for one reason. To lend a hand to grape farmers who find themselves caught between the Volstead Act and their way of life.

"What are they going to do with the excess?" Before the words leave my lips, I am already worried over the thought of our family wine being left to sour and turn. Zinfandel isn't known for its long term cellaring, after all. All that work, for nothing. My shoulders slump at the thought of it.

"They have a warehouse to store it, but..." Matteo dips his head along with his voice.

"But, what?"

"Like I said, I've struck a deal with the church leader, the one who is to manage our wine. He's a real magician."

My eyebrows converge in question.

"He may not be able to turn water into wine." An arrogant smirk stretches my brother's lips, summoning a sense of trepidation in my previously steady knees. "But he can certainly turn perfectly legal Holy Wine into contraband, and he's agreed to sell me some."

"Why on earth would you want to buy back our own wine?"

Matteo tilts his chin up in pompous defiance as I do my best to make sense of what he's getting at.

My stomach sinks and my mouth fills with the taste of something bitter I can't bear to swallow. A hand flies to my mouth as realization dawns on me. Shaking my head back and forth in protest does little save for bringing an even bigger smile to my brother's lips.

I raise my voice, determined to be heard. "No, you can't. It's against the law, and—and, you are the law. You'd be going against all the things you've sworn to uphold as a police officer."

"Lower your voice," Matteo hisses in my direction. "I've spotted an opportunity and I'm going to seize it."

I take a step back, bumping into the vines and finding myself trapped. "You can't do this. Father will be furious when he finds out you are thinking of getting involved with the black market."

"I don't plan on telling him." His gaze turns hard, eliciting an icy shiver up my spine. "And neither will you."

Six

AUGUST 1955
ELKO, NEVADA

JUNE

SEVERAL MINUTES HAVE PASSED. I LET MY encouraging words regarding Meg's potential redemption settle between us, hoping the woman will pick up the torch with me, but knowing, in this moment, nothing is certain. The air in the room grows heavy as we sit in silence. The woman's gaze has shifted from her hands to across the room. She stares, her expression blank, toward the lonely window in the small living room, its view partially concealed by the half-closed curtains. Having seen the lackluster yard beyond, I can't imagine what she finds interesting now, but I follow her gaze anyway, hoping to see something compelling enough to have sequestered her attention.

I've yet to master the art of sitting quietly, so I press on, determined to make our time together mean something. Flipping pages in my notebook, I reread everything I've written there. My concise, angled script lines the pages detailing the archived articles, the court reports, and everything else I could get my hands on about Meg's case.

I even convinced the county clerk to let me have a peek at the big red book. The one documenting Meg's entry and exit to and from jail. Her script-like but legible signature, signed on the day she was released, struck me then. I could tell, in an instant, Meg was an educated woman which convinced me that she knew precisely what she was doing. The signature alone, full and written with a smooth hand, told me more about the supposed criminal than anything else did. From that moment on, I wanted to know how she ended up as a convicted bootlegger.

I knew I had something then, despite the archives indicating no reason as to why a woman in her forties, who surely made a living for herself prior to Prohibition, ended up in a bootleg ring and eventually in jail. She remained silent for a reason, and I'm eager to know why. Even before the devastating years of the Great Depression, where desperate times called for desperate measures, Meg chose to disregard the laws of the Volstead Act, and set her life on what I imagine was a completely different path. Given her association as the Bootleg Queen of Elko, I assume she was proficient at the role too. I could have reasoned that because of hardship or life circumstance one might veer toward criminal activity, but in Meg's case, I haven't been able to understand why.

Meg's stare remains fixed on the window so I allow her a few more minutes' peace while I contemplate where to go from here. I make additional notes on a fresh page, busying myself by describing her lackluster living quarters, thinking perhaps there'll be a space in the article to add insight into the life Meg is living now. As my pencil flows over the page, I reflect on what possessed me to track her down and convince her to talk to me. Perhaps my being here is as much of an oddity as her continued silence is.

Several more minutes later, I have read through my notes three times over. Perhaps she is waiting for me. I consider this as the reason for her silence. I proceed, certain my voice chattering on about what I know of the case will rouse her from her thoughts. Doing my best, I focus on keeping the conversation light and respectful, a handsome task when speaking of one's incarceration.

I consider the timeline of events before voicing what I know to be true. "Meg, from what I've gathered, you were arrested at the warehouse, but it wasn't until weeks later that you were charged and then pled guilty. The case was before the court in no time, and by March you were sent off to serve your sentence." I stop at the mention of her sentence, looking up from my notes in anticipation of receiving a response.

I twirl my pencil between my fingers. Meg remains silent and all I can think is, the woman must need more time to mull my words over. I am in no hurry to be on the receiving end of her sharp tongue again. Instead, I give her some space and bow my head to jot down another flurry of additional questions while I wait her out.

Keeping tabs on her, I glance in her direction every few minutes but cannot catch her eye. She must be deeply lost in thought. I'm about to brush it off as being understandable, given the memories I am asking her to dredge up, when panic grips me. I freeze, my eyes glued to Meg's unmoving form.

What if this isn't intense contemplation? What if the woman is in the middle of some sort of episode? I feel my heart rate quicken at the awareness of such a situation and consider my options. My father's words, warning me that my little adventure to Elko was an ill thought out plan, swirl through my mind.

I summon the courage to try again. I say her name. Clear and a touch louder than the small room dictates. "Meg?" No response.

My eyes dart about the space, taking in the telephone on the side table beside the sofa. At least I can call for help if it is needed. I check my watch, noting the time and realize little more than five minutes have passed. I am conscious of the need to not overreact—some people are more easily lost in thought than others. Perhaps Meg is one of them.

Unable to let the minutes simply tick by, I place my notebook on the sofa and stand, hoping the movement will snap her out of whatever trance has a hold on her.

Nothing.

I step around the coffee table and lean closer while keeping my distance. Her eyes remain open and ah, yes, that was definitely a blink. "Okay, she is fine." The words accompany a quiet exhale that is intended to settle my own nerves.

I take another step closer while positioning myself so as not to be in striking distance should the woman startle when disturbed.

"Meg? Mrs. Bruno? Are you all right? Can I get you something? A glass of water, perhaps?" The woman is unresponsive.

Seven

MEG

I STARE BLANKLY AT THE GIRL STANDING IN FRONT of me. The concern etched into her furrowed brow makes me wonder how long I've been lost in the memories of the past.

"I'm fine." My mouth is as dry as my words are flat. "And stop calling me Mrs. Bruno. I can't stand the designation."

Looking unconvinced and somewhat out of sorts with my retort, June returns to her seat on the sofa. "My apologies, Meg. As I was saying, I'd like to start with a bit of background."

Feeling out of step with the conversation and not knowing what I've missed, I respond with a single nod.

"We've established the newspapers did not print all the details. Correct me if I'm wrong, but it seems as though you didn't speak to the charges laid against you."

My eyes narrow on the girl and her eagerly poised pencil, both of them feeling equally sharp at the moment.

"Not in court, nor to a single reporter," she presses further with eyebrows ready to lift alongside her accusatory comment.

"Is there a question in all of that rambling, missy?" Rough edges take time to smooth, I remind myself with a sharp internal reprimand. But, in this moment, they are the thorn in my side with every word I utter coming out like a bark rather than resembling a conversational tone. I will myself to try harder to be polite.

June seems to brace herself against my insolence, and I feel a prick of guilt at having made her uncomfortable again.

"I—I am simply wondering how the newspapers were expected to record a correct account of the situation if you made no attempt to speak with any of the reporters or even to the judge himself?"

The girl has a point, and it's one I find hard to dismiss, but I am not about to let her know that. "How was I expected to trust the lot of them? They couldn't even spell my name correctly." My words land with a thud at her feet. "How was I supposed to trust anyone at the time?"

How am I supposed to trust you now?

My decision to speak with the girl wavers dangerously inside of me.

"Is that the reason you changed your name?" June flips a few pages back in her notebook. "You were arrested and charged as Mariagrazia Brunelli, but when I first tried to locate you, well, I'll admit, it took some digging before I discovered your name had been changed to Meg Bruno. I assumed at the time that Bruno was your married name?"

I huff a dismissive breath. "I changed my name for the

obvious reason of not wanting my conviction to follow me everywhere I went for the rest of my life. Apparently, that did me little good, since you certainly found your way here." I hear the snark in my voice and frown.

June remains silent as my misplaced outrage settles between us.

"Look." Attempting to reel back my agitation, I try again to explain how I ended up where I am. "The Brunelli name meant little to me by the time I was released from jail so I decided to take a page out of my brother's book, hoping to draw less attention to myself. It's hard enough being a spinster in this town, let alone having my name dragged through the mud on a daily basis just because residents aren't able to forget about it. The rumor mill in a place like this runs twenty-four-seven."

I push down the memory of mothers hauling their small children to the opposite side of the street when they saw me coming as if I was the devil dressed in women's clothes.

"Best I could do was try to remove some of the fuel from the flame of gossip. Over time, people forgot about Maria-grazia Brunelli and with the abolishment of Prohibition, eventually, I carved out a small existence where I wasn't shunned every time I ventured to the market."

"I see." June scratches her pencil against the page of her notebook, recording what I've said for posterity's sake. "You never married?"

"No."

June says nothing, and instead places both her hands on top of her notebook, waiting patiently for me to elaborate since she clearly doesn't believe me.

"Fine. I was engaged once, but he died unexpectedly. It was a long time ago. Before all of this stuff to do with Prohibition and bootlegging." I point toward a small framed portrait tucked neatly out of sight in the small built-in cubby positioned within the wall separating the living room from the kitchen.

June stands to examine the photo more closely. "May I?" She gestures to the cubby and photo frame beyond and waits for me to acknowledge my consent before picking it up to examine it. "He is handsome."

I smile at her remark, remembering the hope I used to see shining in his eyes. "He was."

"How did he die?" June asks as she replaces the frame and takes her seat again.

"Farming accident." After all this time, I am surprised by the sudden wave of emotion I feel when talking about those early years. "He was determined to make something of himself. I suppose we all were at that age. His name was Lorenzo, and he promised me we would marry just as soon as he saved enough for his own piece of land. It would have been a simple life, being a farmer's wife. We were young and in love, and I embraced everything, believing I was so close to having it all."

"I'm sorry."

"Me too." I meet her eyes. "I imagine my life would have turned out very different had I married Lorenzo."

June changes tracks after allowing me a moment to reflect on my loss. "You mentioned your brother. Have you stayed in touch with your family, then?"

"No."

I can tell the girl wants more. Thankfully, I've become accustomed to not always giving others what they want.

June clears her throat, making me wonder if I should offer her something to drink again. Not wishing to be turned down twice in two hours, I decide better of it. Instead, I force myself to stand and step the three paces toward the small black fan on top of the metal TV tray and flip it on. I take in the tray's once vibrant floral motif, faded and scratched from frequent use as the fan whirs to life, sending warm air circulating about the room. I pause and consider how much I, myself, resemble the battered up TV tray.

I amble back to my chair, adjusting the pillow at my back before meeting the girl's expectant eyes with a heavy dose of reluctance.

"Is it true you didn't speak up for yourself in court or with any such reporter about the events that took place in January 1926?"

"I did not."

"Meg." June places both elbows on top of her knees and leans forward, resting her chin on her entwined knuckles. "Can I ask you why you chose not to defend yourself? I can understand why you might not speak to the reporters, but to the judge? Surely, you would have been afforded the opportunity to mount a defense."

June's question begs for a sensible reply. The truth is, I was compelled to remain silent. George's impassioned face appears in my mind's eye. A few months after meeting him, the man became my everything. Needing little convincing, I fell into his bed and into his business. I trusted him implicitly, and in turn he trusted me with his operation, a sign that, to me, meant he respected me enough to be on equal footing.

"Maria," he had told me in slightly accented English, "the first rule of being a bootlegger is, above all else, you protect the tribe." He had grasped my hands in his and pulled me close, peering into my eyes with an intensity so severe I swear I felt it in my soul. "Then you protect the merchandise." My mistake was in assuming his fierce attention on me was love.

Shaking my head to free the memory, I search for a response suitable to satiate June's hunger for knowledge while holding the real reason close to my chest, at least until I can be sure the girl is worthy of the truth and my story. I attempt the nonchalance of a shrug but feel the delivery fall flat. "The authorities caught me red-handed. I was in the middle of a warehouse, surrounded by barrels and crates of wine. What would you have had me say?"

"Forgive my ignorance on the subject." June lifts her shoulders, conveying her lack of understanding. "I'm trying to understand why you were charged with selling alcohol to minors, and not at all charged with being in possession of hundreds of gallons of prohibited wine."

The girl is quicker than I gave her credit for and proves once more her prowess as a reporter is serving her well. "It wasn't uncommon for officers of the law to find it hard to believe a woman could be involved in such illegal activity. Regardless of whether or not I was found among the contraband, they assumed women were incapable of betraying the laws of Prohibition."

"I don't understand." June's head quirks to the left.

I feel my lips curve a fraction, remembering the reason for my unofficial title of Bootleg Queen. "I lost count of the number of times I outsmarted the local police. Even the sheriff was no match for me. When the dry agents arrived in town, I developed a fresh approach, which allowed me to evade the feds a time or two, and they were the tenacious sort."

I raise my eyebrows in June's direction. "In the early

days, nobody expected a middle-aged woman to be hauling black market booze across state lines. It was unheard of for women to do such things. They simply couldn't believe we were capable of these lawless acts. Add to that, it was illegal in many states for a police officer to search a woman. It made for an excellent ruse, don't you think? Besides, it was exciting as hell to sidle up to an officer of the law with contraband hidden in the vehicle and give him a sweet smile and be sent on my way with a 'have a nice day, ma'am.'"

Understanding dawns across the girl's features, and her face lights up with a knowing smile. "That's how you became known as the Bootleg Queen."

My mind drifts back to the first time I heard the words, *Bootleg Queen*.

Eight

NOVEMBER 1922
ELKO, NEVADA

MEG

I HADN'T REALIZED HE WAS REFERRING TO ME AT first. George gathered us together at the warehouse, each of us pulling up a crate or bale of hay to lean against as we waited for our fearless leader to speak. I had only been with the boys for a matter of months, but with every successful run, our trust in, and care for, one another grew stronger by the day.

Eyeing the room, his serious expression morphed into a wide grin. His hand held a glass of whiskey in what I assumed was a readiness to toast a recent success. "Boys." His piercing eyes landed on me. "And lady. Let me tell you a story." Having been given the go ahead, Carlo, George's right-hand man, passed around glasses and filled them with a solid three finger pour of what George liked to refer to as the good stuff. I remember thinking, something really must have pleased him to offer the whole gang this kind of generosity.

CHAPTER EIGHT

"Someone among us has crossed over the threshold into notoriety." He teased us by drawing out what he'd gathered us there to say. "A right accomplishment, if you ask me."

One of the boys heckled him from the back of the warehouse, telling him to stop grandstanding and get on with it. George just chuckled and waved him off, the warmth of our mutual companionship growing to a fever pitch after another successful day of work.

"One of our best customers sought me out to thank me for the whiskey that showed up on the shelves of a local speakeasy this afternoon, since they saw the car get pulled over by a Prohibition officer just outside of town this morning." Chuckling at his own shenanigans, George lifted his glass in my direction, forgoing a lengthy explanation. "I heard the reference for the first time today, and it's a feather in our cap, to be sure. Boys, we have in our midst the Bootleg Queen of Elko, Nevada." All heads swiveled in my direction and George followed up with a toast to me, to Maria, the Bootleg Queen.

What followed was a slew of questions and comments, all of them coming at me rapid fire. "How'd you do it, Maria?" Carlo asked, leaning his stocky frame toward me for the secret.

"Did that agent give you any trouble, cause you know I'll deck him if he did." Lewis teased while flexing his biceps.

"Way to go, Maria. Let's raise a glass to the prettiest bootlegger in all of Nevada."

The night flew by as we toasted and boasted of our achievements. Backs were slapped and hugs were exchanged. Through it all, George stood off to the side, sipping his whiskey, watching, and letting me immerse myself in the knowledge that I had earned my place among them. I knew then, if called to do so, I would do anything for any one of them. After my father discovered my bootlegging activities and disowned me, George's crew gave me the only thing I was desperate for—a home and a family.

Nine

AUGUST 1955

ELKO, NEVADA

MEG

I LOOK UP TO SEE JUNE'S BODY AS SHE ANGLES forward, waiting for my response. "That's it. Am I right? Is that how you became known as the Bootleg Queen?"

"In the end, yes. Things didn't exactly start out that way, though." I tuck the small piece of pride I secretly covet over the title out of sight, not wishing to appear overindulgent with such mentions.

The girl's confusion returns with speed, something clearly not adding up in that quick thinking brain of hers. "The charges, then, of selling alcohol to minors?"

A weighted groan drops my chin toward my chest. "I knew it was risky, but I was outvoted."

I sense June's desire to interrupt and ask by whom? But I continue on, thwarting her curiosity with my own words. One step at a time—she has yet to earn my full trust.

"I originally assumed it was several affluent parents demanding the sheriff do something about the alcohol being sold at the high school when they learned of it, though I can't be certain. Either way, it was about that time when an investigation was brewing in Elko to catch those dealing in the black market. The feds had been called back in and after several months of gathering evidence, everything came to a head on January 12th, 1926 with the raids you've read about in the papers. Three different locations, eight arrests, and almost nine hundred gallons total of illegal alcohol seized in a single day."

"How did they tie you to the minors?" June's hand scribbles with speed over her notebook.

"The students identified me." This is a truthful statement, I reason.

I can't give away all of my secrets.

She lifts her head, looking shocked. "The same students who had been your customers, turned you in?"

"I can't blame them, really." June eyes me, still not convinced, so I take another approach. "Put yourself in their shoes. A parent, likely a father, bearing down on you for bringing shame upon your family name. News like that traveled fast in Elko back in the day. The only way for the students to protect themselves was to point their fingers toward the only person they were acquainted with. The unsuspecting middle-aged woman who brought them the liquor. If it wasn't so devastating to my life, it would almost be funny."

"What would be funny?" June asks.

A beaten down sigh ushers in my humiliation. "The identity that allowed me to break the law for years without getting caught was the same identity that put me in jail, in the end."

Ten

JUNE

"So, they charged you with selling alcohol to minors?" I can hear the incredulity in my voice. "You were sentenced to three hundred and ninety days. That hardly seems like a crime worthy of such jail time."

Meg's voice breaks into a hoarse chuckle which I choose to interpret as an agreement to my statement. "That about sums it up." The old woman's shoulders rise and fall. "With the students' testimonies to back up their charges, there was nothing left for me to say. I had been caught."

"But surely there is more. You can't possibly have earned a title such as the Bootleg Queen of Elko for selling liquor to minors a few times."

"There were several students." Meg levels a pointed look in my direction, and I wonder if she's trying to convince herself or me.

"Yes, but—"

"Eleven of them were called to testify, each one indi-

47

cating I was their first and only contact for the liquor." Meg tucks her chin and lifts her eyebrows at me, and I sense she is trying to get behind this version of the story rather than fess up with the complete truth.

Waving a hand as if to wish it all away, she continues. "All in all, it was a big hullabaloo with prosecutors worrying over the teens being pressured not to testify and such."

"Pressured? By who?" I inch forward on the sofa, certain I've found something I can sink my teeth into.

To this, Meg has no response. A slight shrug of her shoulders confirms my initial suspicion. She isn't being entirely honest with me.

I flip pages of my notebook furiously, looking for the charges I detailed to prepare for this interview. Careful to avoid further mention of newspaper reporter accounts, I decide instead to quote straight from a source Meg can't argue against. "The court record states you were charged and plead guilty to eleven counts of selling alcohol to minors."

"Yes." Meg draws out the word. "Hence the eleven boys who testified against me. One charge for each incident."

I sense her wondering if I am slow to understand this logic, so I try another tactic, nibbling around the edges of what I am seeking. "Would I be correct if I guessed these eleven occurrences were not the only ones?"

Meg's smirk tells me she knows what I am getting at. "You would."

"Would you be willing to elaborate?" I lean back against the sofa cushions, crossing my arms over my chest.

Meg's sigh is exasperated despite her slim offering of details thus far. "Fine. I suppose it won't do any harm now. When they found me in the warehouse, the feds may have guessed at my involvement with other aspects of the operation, but they couldn't prove it. I imagine it was not for lack of trying, though. Instead, it was likely their abysmal track record of succeeding that was the issue." Her eye roll tells me she has little respect for the Prohibition officers or the task force that was brought upon Elko's head in pursuit of bootleggers like her.

"What other aspects of the operation were you involved in?" I may be pushing my luck by asking such a bold question, but I test the waters anyway, hoping Meg will throw me a bone.

"Well, there was the speakeasy, for one." She says it with such nonchalance, I wonder if it's the truth.

"Speakeasy?" I toss her a sideways glance while trying to remain unfazed by her words.

"Nothing fancy, but it was a place of respite for those seeking to imbibe illegal spirits safely." Meg's expression softens as she reminisces. "Given the news of dangerous practices making people blind, or worse, I struck a deal with the producer of the best hooch in the country."

"Who was that?" I ask, more out of a desire to keep her talking than anything else.

Meg's head shakes back and forth, with sadness over something unknown to me lining her features. "I was beside myself when I learned Birdie had blown herself up with that Montana still of hers, but by then I was out of the game, anyway. A few months later, we all were, given the repeal of Prohibition."

I suck in a breath at the realization that Meg knew the infamous Birdie Brown. My eyes scan the room, taking in the meager style in which she lives and I wonder, for the first time, if life prior to her conviction was experienced on a much larger scale than I ever imagined.

"So, your association with the speakeasy made you the Bootleg Queen?" I feel my eyebrows knit together, wanting to get it right.

Meg appears to consider my question. "I suppose, in a roundabout way. If you asked the others, though, I'd wager they'd say it had more to do with my ability to dodge the law. My success rate was higher than anyone else in the crew."

I am tossed up between wanting to know more about the others and where the topic of Meg's life as a Bootleg Queen might lead me. I decide to let her steer our course and wait for her to continue.

I don't have to wait long. When the corner of Meg's lip twitches upward, I swear the energy in the room shifts. Confirmation arrives as the hair on my forearms tingle when she begins to speak.

"One time, me and the boys were hauling a big shipment, more than could fit within the hidden compartments of our automobiles." Meg's head lolls to one side, absorbed by the memory. "This got us thinking. We had this grand notion that if we moved the entire lot at once, we'd avoid the off chance of getting snagged and we could live off the proceeds for months."

Meg dabs at the moisture gathering on her upper lip. "Of course, this was our little pipe dream as we sweated it out in the Nevada sun. That is until George got to thinking about it himself."

Licking my lips, I feel the hum of anticipation vibrate through my body, but given the woman's apparent inability to share the truth with me, I caution my excitement with a hefty dose of suspicion. "George?" I ask, hoping to draw at least this confirmation from our exchange.

"Yes. George Fumagalli. I'm certain if you did any

digging at all, you would have come across his name." Meg lifts an accusatory eyebrow in question before continuing. "So, George." Her voice quavers a little, and I wonder if George is perhaps a sensitive topic.

I jot the name in my notebook, verifying Meg is indeed referring to the elusive George. The one who I know for a fact pled not guilty at the same time as Meg pled guilty and, from what I learned from my research, was notorious for having multiple charges against him at any given time. He apparently used his influence along with his affluence to coerce, bribe, and run out of town anyone who might speak against him in court but, until I heard it from Meg's lips, I couldn't be certain of any of it.

"He decided we should fool the dry agents by doing it like they did in New York City. He was forever full of big ideas. Not that all of them were successful, mind you." Meg laughs, transforming her appearance from detached to something resembling gleeful.

"For months he planned. He got a business permit from the city to open a funeral parlor, you see."

Meg regards me with a conspiratorial lift of her eyebrows. "He was particularly delighted with himself for pulling that one over on the city with his little scheme. Opening up a false business front to increase his illegal operation." Another chuckle, deep and low, rumbles out of the woman.

"Anyway, with a permit in hand, he and the boys outfitted the front of the shop with plush furnishings and dim lighting, you know the kind that'd be suitable and pass for that type of place of business if someone was looking to bury a loved one."

I dip my head, encouraging her to continue.

"He bought a hearse and began reinforcing it for the extra weight it was going to carry. I don't know how much money he sank into the venture, but that thing was ready to carry more than we'd ever transported at one time before. Then there was the coffin. Lined with plush, silky fabric fit for a king or, as George preferred to say, thick enough to protect the merchandise."

Meg shifts in her chair, her posture relaxing further as she talks.

"The day comes." The surly woman who, only an hour ago, wasn't inclined to give me the time of day, comes alive with sparkling eyes and a genuine smile. "We all have our marching orders. George drives the hearse as the rest of us take our usual cars and trucks, scattering around the back roads and varying our routes to pick up the delivery."

I resist the urge to write the story down and instead keep my attention locked on Meg.

"We load up. No issues whatsoever. Nobody's been tailed, tracked, or spotted. George takes the bulk of the delivery in the hearse, hiding it in the specialized compartments before loading the more expensive lot into the empty coffin waiting in the back of the hearse." A hand covers Meg's mouth as she stifles a laugh.

"Knowing all too well that waiting around is just asking for trouble, we moved quickly before falling into line. George and his loaded down hearse lead the way back to town and the funeral parlor where he planned to unload the delivery for safekeeping and distribution."

"Oh my. That is clever." I agree.

"Each of us followed close behind at the snail's pace of an actual funeral procession. As we arrived at the city limits, we encountered other vehicles on the road. Just as planned, they slowed for us and allowed the procession to pass. We drove right past city hall and the sheriff's building and that is when things went sideways."

Meg pauses her storytelling, raising her eyebrows for emphasis.

"I was riding in the car three back from the hearse, dressed in my Sunday best in an effort to really sell the ruse when the sheriff, at the time, pulls out in front of George and waves for him to follow. At first, I think we're busted. My driver, Carlo, George's right-hand man and a genuinely kind soul, starts contemplating pulling out and heading for an escape route. I could tell he was worried about being busted with me in the car beside him. Loyal to a fault, Carlo was. George was always his first concern, but I ran a close second."

Meg's smile is wide and sincere at the mention of Carlo, and I find myself smiling right along with her.

She shifts in her chair before meeting my eyes. "I placed a calming hand on his broad forearm and reminded him of the plan. We had already decided ahead of time to keep the usual bootleg vehicles out of the mix, my steadfast truck included. I told him we were dressed for the part, so we might as well see it through."

I lean in, engrossed in her tale.

"We crawled through town at a snail's pace, the sheriff's car continuing to guide us all the way. Let me tell you."

Meg's hand slices through the air with emphasis. "There is simply nothing more unsettling to a long line of lawbreakers than a leisurely stroll through downtown with the sheriff at the helm."

Shaking her head in disbelief, she continues. "So, the sheriff heads toward the Elko cemetery, but George flags him down and tells him we are heading to the Tuscarora Cemetery instead. The sheriff insists on providing his escort, and we travel the fifty miles out of town to a cemetery none of us had ever seen before, hoping there is an empty mound of earth waiting for us when we arrive."

My mouth falls open.

"Thankfully, luck was on our side that day and there was a grave just waiting for some poor Tuscarora resident and his party of mourners to arrive."

"What did you do?"

Meg can't hold back her laughter any longer. "We had no other choice but to bury the coffin loaded with top shelf liquor, say a few prayers, and thank the sheriff for his help."

"But what about the other funeral?" I ask, while trying to hold back a giggle of my own.

Meg's laugh erupts an octave louder. "We bribed a grave digger to cover our tracks and hightailed it out of there as quickly as we could so we wouldn't be caught. I can tell you one thing, though. It was a miracle that the coffin's fabric lining was enough to dampen the sound of sloshing liquor and rattling glass, since the boys struggled against the weight of it as they lowered it into the ground. The whole time, the sheriff stood there out of respect for the deceased, hat in hand with a bowed head, paying his respects to a casket full of Prohibition alcohol."

I lift my pencil, ready to record the story into my notebook.

"I am pretty sure George shed actual tears that day." Meg's laugh settles like the patter of a rain storm transforming into a sprinkle. "I think that was his one and only funeral. I never knew what happened to the hearse or the rest of it. All I know is, he never lived it down, at least not for as long as I knew him."

Meg grows quiet and I take the opportunity to record her entertaining story as quickly as I can. Using the shorthand I've become accustomed to while engaged in interviews, I write furiously, determined not to miss a thing.

"What are you doing?" Meg's voice turns on me, startling me from my focus.

"I want to get this down before I forget. You told such a lively story. I am certain I can find a place for it within the article."

"You will do no such thing." Meg barks.

I lift my head to find her hard gaze on me. "Excuse me?"

"I did not give you permission to print what I've said." Meg dismisses me by shifting her eyes toward the window, acting as though I am no longer in the room with her.

Checking the time on my watch, I note the dinner hour is upon us. Though the sun isn't likely to set for another two hours, I had planned to be back at my motel room in time for an early bedtime. The drive and sweltering heat of the day has done plenty to wear me out this evening.

At this rate, it will be Christmas before I get anything resembling a front-page story from the woman. I promised my parents I'd be home in three days. Tapping the eraser end of my pencil against my lips, I consider my options. Maybe I could find another angle to this story. I can't force the woman if she isn't inclined. I try to wrap my head around the problem, but all I circle back to is Meg's resistance. There is no other option. I'll have to find another way.

"Meg, you agreed to let me proceed. Otherwise, what am I doing here?" I try my best to keep the agitation from my voice, but my patience is wearing thin and my stomach, now grumbling its displeasure, needs sustenance. "If you aren't able to share what can be printed, I'm afraid we're out of time. I came to hear your story and write an article. If I can't write the article then I might as well head home now."

"You are hungry." She announces it rather than asks. "I'll fix us something to eat."

Eleven

MEG

I AM OUT OF MY CHAIR AND SHUFFLING TOWARD
the kitchen before the girl can stop me. Willing my body not
to betray me, I move fast, thankful to have a few quick
strides left in me. I sense June's frustration at another delay
and my refusal to grant her access to the one piece of information I've given her all day. My lack of cooperation has put
the girl in a sour mood.

Carrying my sad offering of crackers with a dollop of
mayonnaise, now crusted yellow by a day spent in the heat
and garnished with a slice of less than pleasant smelling
Spam, I can tell the girl is ready to call it a night. She is
closing her notebook and reaching for the bag at her feet as I
return to the living room.

Placing the plate in front of her on the coffee table, I
avoid her eyes but offer a compromise. "Let's keep the story
off the record for now and then decide later if it will be
included."

The girl nods her head and places her bag back on the floor, acquiescing on the topic. "Alright. I can agree to that."

I decide to pass on taking a cracker, and instead return to my chair before asking, "What's next?"

I feel compelled to toss the girl a bone. Feeling a touch sheepish about my waffling stance on whether I will give her what she's come here for, I try to smooth things over.

"You know, there was this one time when I was bringing in a delivery of wine from California and my tire blew out." I offer what I hope is a slight smile in the girl's direction. "There I was on the side of a dirt road with a trunk full of wine crates. I was sure when the local police pulled up behind me, I was done in for since the tire iron and spare were in the trunk. Only thing was, they were buried under the crates of wine. My options were limited, as I'm sure you can imagine."

I glance up to find June listening, but sense she is still reeling from the heat of my sharp reprimand over the funeral procession.

"In order to fix the tire"—I give the girl a shrewd look—"which I knew how to do. I would have had to unload the wine to the side of the road and retrieve the tire and iron. I was leaning against the back of the trunk, considering my options when a police officer came to a stop behind me."

June reclines against the sofa cushions, crossing her arms over her chest. The notebook and pencil remain untouched beside her, and I note the tinge of youthful sass lining her features. I'm losing the girl, I can feel it.

Unsettled is the predominant emotion running around within the confines of my head. On the one hand, I'd be happy to let the girl leave. Heck, I might even walk her to the door with a spring in my step if I knew for sure doing so was the right thing. On the other hand, seeing her and knowing what I know, I am eager to have her stay. If only she can be patient with me as I gather my courage. I keep talking, hoping my words are enough to convince her to stay. "The officer gets out of his car and greets me, asking how I am and such before bending down to examine my tire. I put on my most pleasant smile and tell him…"

"I don't mean to interrupt, Meg, but if this is another one of your stories that I won't be able to include in the article, I'm not sure I need to hear it."

My chin inches down as I avoid June's expectant gaze. "I understand."

Thoughts, all of them at odds with one another, race through my mind. How will I find the courage to confide in this girl? My instincts tell me I can trust her, but they've steered me wrong before. What good are instincts if you can't rely on them for even the simplest of situations?

If only it was a straightforward story to tell with a beginning, a middle, and an end. I suppose all stories, at the heart of them, are simple. It's the emotions that bring the challenging bits into the mix.

I steal a peek at June from beneath my downcast eyes. She is waiting expectantly, and I can't fault her for it. She doesn't know it yet, but there is a war zone of emotions we will have to go through to get to a semblance of anything being right again. I am not too late to try again. I nudge the hope of self-redemption back into my line of sight, forcing myself to keep my eyes on the ball.

What the girl likely assumes is simply a story, and a front-page one at that, is the entirety of my life. Having it be reduced to a fleeting mention doesn't sit well with me. Today's newspaper lines tomorrow's waste bin, after all. I feel the tickle of uncertainty creep into my throat. If I am to do this, I will need more than a handful of gumption, and a determined young girl, coaxing the details one by one into the light of day.

Easing myself out of the chair, I catch the shadow of disappointment as it falls across June's face. "Don't fret your pretty little head," I tell June in my gravelly voice. "I'm doing my best to tell you my story, but I'm gonna need a drink for this." I flip on two lamps, illuminating the room in a soft glow of orange.

"Oh." The girl relaxes a fraction while leaning her back into the sofa cushions once more.

"Can I fix you one?" The humor is not lost on me as I attempt to play the unfamiliar role of a good hostess. "I don't have much, but whiskey is a staple in this house."

June checks her watch, and I wonder if she is only used to cocktail hour on Friday nights. Or perhaps she is seeking another way to turn down my offer and hightail it out of here.

"Well, I suppose one drink couldn't hurt," she smiles. "It is a might bit later than I realized. The day is getting on toward half past seven already. I don't wish to overstay my welcome."

I chuckle at her politeness wrapped in societal niceties as I totter a few steps forward. I expect Miss Monroe and I could both learn something from one another. My gaze falls to the plate of ill-scented crackers still sitting on the coffee table, their mayonnaise and Spam combo doing little to spur an appetite. Lifting the plate, I carry it to the kitchen and toss its contents into the waste bin. No sense inadvertently poisoning the girl with a poorly constructed snack.

At least the girl is staying. I stand on tiptoe and reach for the whiskey in the tall cupboard above the sink. My finger-tips grace the smooth glass but do little to seize the bottle. Retracting my arm, I scan the kitchen counter for something useful. I retrieve a well-worn spatula from a drawer, doing my best to ignore the reason I pushed the whiskey bottle a touch further out of easy reach several weeks ago.

Even before the test results were in, the doctor cautioned me at our last meeting that alcohol and cigarettes were not the companions of a life long lived. Little did he realize I wasn't looking to extend my life. No, I'm simply trying to survive the pain of the every day. And for that, alcohol and cigarettes have served me well for years.

Whiskey bottle in hand, I place my best two glasses on the counter before reaching into the icebox for the tray of ice cubes. The ice cubes clink against the glass, sending me back to another time when laughter rang through the air and the excitement of a love affair was only heightened by the real threat of being discovered by Prohibition officials.

Twelve

OCTOBER 1925

ELKO, NEVADA

MEG

IT WAS 1925 AND OUR BOOTLEGGING OPERATION was flourishing. The high life of Prohibition, speakeasies, and the thrill of skirting the law has felt just out of my reach these past three years since I hooked up with George and his crew. Seldom do we visit a speakeasy, save for The Bluff, and that hardly counts since I own the joint.

Perhaps I assumed my life would be filled with more adventure as a bootlegger. The flappers and the gents certainly manage to frolic here, there, and everywhere in a bustle of glitter, jazz, and champagne. Our life, it seems, revolves around bootleg runs, managing the crew, and accounting for the whole lot.

A weary sigh slips past my red painted lips. Another successful haul is sure to have George in a good mood. I wouldn't dream of begrudging him the time to bask in his success, but I wonder if there is any point to it, if we aren't able to enjoy ourselves, that is.

CHAPTER TWELVE

"Hey, Maria." George calls up to me from the hay-strewn warehouse floor.

I push my sour disposition aside and insert a playful tone. "Stop your hollering. I'm in the loft, not Timbuktu."

His good-natured chuckle arrives ahead of his stocky physical form on the loft's ladder. Though he is a few years older than my forty-six years, the demands of daily life keep him strong and limber. Stepping in my direction, the scent of hay alights while the dust motes are stirred into the air by his movement.

The ice clatters against the tumbler as I drop an ice-picked, irregular shaped piece of frozen water into each of the two waiting glasses.

"What's all this?" George presses his body against my back while wrapping his arms around my waist. I inhale his scent as his body curves against mine. "I thought we were going to go over the accounts."

I deliver a coy smile over my shoulder, catching his afternoon stubble against my cheek. "You know we hardly have a moment alone anymore with all the boys coming and going. Things have gotten busy around here. All work and no play make George a dreary boy." I tease him with my words.

"I'm beginning to like the sound of this." He nuzzles his agreement of the situation into my hair, and I feel my body respond, as any space between us is swallowed up by anticipation.

Pouring from the whiskey bottle that has been resting on the makeshift counter of a piece of wood resting on top of a few hay bales, I pass a glass in his direction. "Cheers," I say, meeting his gaze as he bypasses the drink and dips his lips to meet mine.

Thirteen

AUGUST 1955

ELKO, NEVADA

MEG

"DO YOU NEED A HAND IN THERE?" JUNE'S VOICE inquires, pulling me from my reverie with a jolt.

"I'm fine." The exertion I am using to remove the bottle's well-placed stopper while simultaneously tamping down my vivid recollection of George has me seeing double.

Placing the bottle between my arthritic knees, I tug and twist the bottle's top with gnarled fingers. Frustration lines my mumbled profanities and for the hundredth time today, I curse my body's inability to keep the process of growing old from my awareness.

"Got you." The stopper releases as perspiration slips down my back from the effort.

Tilting the bottle of brown liquid, the familiar scent of wood and peat rise up to greet me as I eyeball a two finger pour into each glass. I pull an old wooden serving tray from a bottom cupboard and place both glasses on top of it.

CHAPTER THIRTEEN

Adding a bowl of potato chips and two cold glasses of water from the jug in the fridge fills up the tray.

I note my meager offering, now wishing I had made more of an effort and gotten the girl lemonade or iced tea for the August heat that is refusing to release its grip despite the evening hour. Try as I might, I can't help but feel the prick of a growing kinship with June. She did admit her shortcomings as a reporter, and I sense she believes redemption, where I am concerned, is possible. Perhaps this is a good place to start. If she can find the patience, maybe I'll find the strength.

I lift the tray and move toward the living room, the clinking of glasses announcing my presence. I wish I was as certain as her youthful exuberance seems to be. This, perhaps, is what unsettles me most. I could still beg forgiveness and send her on her way. She may be miffed at me for a short time, but it is the only way I know to be assured the pain will end with me. Having spent the afternoon with the girl, I've really no desire to disrupt her life for the sake of my salvation.

June makes room for the tray on the coffee table by stacking old editions of *Life* magazine and the scrapbook I neglected to tuck out of sight into one pile at the table's far side.

"Thank you," I say as I settle the tray on the table. I take my glass of whiskey and retreat to my corner of the room, well aware the girl won't wait on me forever.

Fourteen

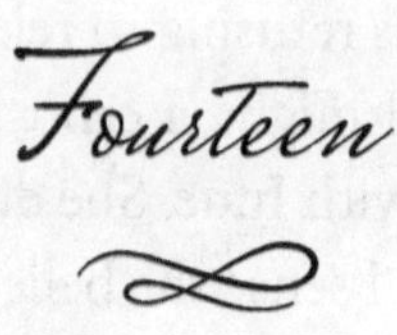

JUNE

I LIFT THE GLASS TO MY LIPS AND TAKE A SMALL SIP. The brown liquid burns its way across my tongue and down my throat. Aware there is little food in my stomach, I take a potato chip, its crunch filling the silence in the small room.

Looking for a way to take the pressure off of Meg, I pursue a new line of questioning. "What can you tell me about the others arrested on the same day?" Placing my glass on the coffee table, I open my notebook, determined to get this interview going. "I believe there were eight of you over three raids. Does that sound right?"

Meg sips her whiskey before searching the ceiling for an answer. I presume she is tallying the names in her head, each one of them a person she knew and not merely a number reported in a newspaper or a court document. "Yes, there were eight of us in total." Her head bobs up and down in a slow, considering movement.

I am walking on eggshells, mindful not to press too hard or too fast. Tossing all of my assumptions about Meg, along with a handful of my originally crafted, but clearly useless, questions out the window, I set about to create a pathway of events that I can shape into something resembling a narrative.

"Did you know all the men involved?" Again, not wishing to fall on the sword of assumption, I ask a question whether or not I am certain I know the answer.

Meg shifts in her chair, and I resolve to pay closer attention to her body language in an effort to head off any future disagreements before they rise.

"I knew all the men. Some better than others, of course. Carlo, as I mentioned before, was George's right-hand man. He was a short, burly man with a tender heart. He and his new wife lived in a small two-story house in town."

She takes another sip of whiskey. "Carlo stayed close to George, partly for the sake of his job but also, I suspect, out of duty to the man who gave him a break when he desperately needed one. Then there was Lewis. He was the muscle." The corner of Meg's lip twitches up. "Lewis was most likely to be called when a large shipment needed moving or when a head needed to roll."

Meg's hand waves dismissively as if the thought of men brawling is standard business practice. "Didn't happen often since George maintained good relations with those on both sides of the law but every once in a while, Lewis was more than happy to oblige."

A look of contemplation crosses over Meg's face. "Course, I never figured out if Lewis actually enjoyed the action of a fisticuff or the extra pay George offered him when things came to a head. That man was forever up to his eyeballs in gambling debt, so I'm certain the extra money bailed Lewis out of a scrape or two. We were all local to the area, though some lived on the outskirts of town on farms and such. The logic was it was far easier to make and hide liquor away from prying eyes on a farm with a remote location."

After making a note, I lift my head and catch the slightest hint of a smile playing at the corners of Meg's mouth. I tilt my head in question and wait for her to enlighten me.

"The men always thought they were the brightest of the bunch, more intelligent than me, that is. They were the ones who planned and schemed, determined to outsmart anyone in a uniform. Their confidence in themselves made them certain they were one step ahead of both the law and the sole woman among them." Meg's shoulders lift in a *what are you going to do about it* gesture.

"We were a family of sorts. As is often the case with family, we each had our place among the lot with our own share of disagreements. I was the little sister of the group, despite being older than a few of them. They liked me well enough. Well enough, I suppose, to let me handle the accounts, which I was quite good at, so long as I followed their lead otherwise. They simply presumed to think they knew what was best, regardless of the question at hand." Meg shakes her head. "I told you earlier I had been outvoted about the business of selling liquor to those kids."

"Yes." I curb my body's eagerness to lean forward.

"Truth is, I was often outvoted. It's why I preferred to do my bootleg runs alone. The boys leaned into the tactic of posturing and decoys. When they wanted me to do something their way, they plied me with platitudes, telling me that with my track record, I was the only one who could go in undetected. Stroked my emotions by saying I could pull off looking like someone's mother and would easily go undetected. Despite my many contributions to the business end of things, they couldn't shift their perspective from thinking of me as their little sister. They assumed their thoughts and ideas were the only ones and there was rarely room for discussion when I had something to contribute."

Meg's sigh is laced with impatience, and it's a sentiment I recognize within my life as well. The impatience of forever being told how and what to do by the men I am surrounded by. All I have to do is think back to the heated discussion that ensured I did not leave my family home on pleasant terms with my father when I set out to travel to Elko this morning. His insistence that I squash my stubbornness and at least meet the man he believes is my one true love sits like a stone in my stomach. This mystery man, my father is convinced, is surely the one to save me from a life as a dreaded reporter. I fumed in silence while holding my tongue, wordlessly trying to convince him that being a reporter isn't as dangerous as he thinks and having a husband will only slow me down.

My sigh matches Meg's. Of course, those weren't his exact words, I admit in silent indignation. I remember something about him having arranged a time for the man to join our family for dinner one night this week and my impromptu trip out of town was causing him embarrassment, as dinner would have to be rescheduled.

In a subdued tone, Meg continues, wrenching me from

my thoughts. "They never came around to understanding the way I hid in plain sight. But you know, until the day the raids snagged us all, I had never been arrested before. That is not something any of them could claim."

"What do you mean by hiding in plain sight?" My pencil is poised and itching to write, sensing a nugget is about to be dropped in my lap.

"I lived at the center of town, in a little apartment above the speakeasy. The entire building was decked out as a perfume manufacturing company. A solid front for the speakeasy and boldly located around the corner from the police station and city hall. It was never raided. In fact, I'm not sure they ever suspected it as a place of ill repute." Meg's laugh falls short. "I returned there the day I was released from jail. Not a thing had been touched. Everything, save for the stores of liquor that George's boys likely removed, was just as I had left it when I went to the warehouse on the morning of the raids."

"They didn't suspect you at all, you mean?" I lean back against the sofa, considering this new piece of information.

"Not the feds, it seems. At first, I thought I had imagined the shock on the two Prohibition agent's faces that day at the warehouse, but upon returning to the apartment after months away, I realized they weren't expecting to find me there that day."

My brow crinkles. "If you hadn't been at the warehouse, you wouldn't have been arrested then?"

Meg's lips purse in response. "I can't prove that." She pauses a moment. "But I suspect as much."

"Then how did they connect you with selling liquor to minors?"

Meg lets out a slow exhale. "That's a much more difficult question to answer."

The hair on the back of my neck lifts, eliciting a shiver down my spine, despite the stifling warmth of Meg's little house. Something isn't right here. I can feel it with every inch of my body.

Gauging her reluctance to answer more about the charges set against her, I decide to stay on track and learn more about the seven others arrested at the same time. "I've seen several mentions of that man you mentioned earlier. You've referred to him as having a right-hand man in Carlo, so I'm guessing he was the ringleader or something. I'm wondering if you can tell me more about George? He was arrested but pled not guilty and ended up getting off scot-free."

I reach for another chip, feigning ignorance at my awareness that the topic of George may be a harder road to travel where Meg is concerned. I am contemplating the wisdom of this line of questioning with the chip halfway to my mouth but decide to take the risk and add, "I have that correct, right? He is the same George from your story about the funeral procession? George Fumagalli? He was..." I flip the pages of my notebook to find what I am looking for. "Yes, he was an Italian born, American businessman. He was quite enterprising back in the day, owning several legitimate businesses, in addition to what I suspect were his illegal ones, but I don't want to make assumptions here."

Meg sputters her sip of whiskey, and I am rewarded with the knowledge that I've hit the bullseye. There is definitely more to learn about George, it seems. Perhaps he is the key to unlocking whatever Meg is reluctant to share. Watching Meg's reaction, my mind spins with the question of how

George fits in to her conviction and subsequent jail time. Surely, a man of such conniving ways might not bat an eye if it meant saving his own neck.

Meg's sputter turns into a coughing fit, which does neither of us any good. I give her a moment to recover herself, but when she doesn't, I retrieve a glass of water from the tray and move toward her.

Fifteen

AUGUST 1955

ELKO, NEVADA

MEG

"GOODNESS GRACIOUS." THE GIRL SAYS AS SHE moves toward me, her hand outstretched, holding a glass of water in my direction.

My mind races back to a time when I uttered those exact words. Of course, I was batting my eyelashes and pressing a feigned hand to my chest as the police officer cautioned me on the lead foot I'd been using against the automobile's gas pedal. All these memories rising to the surface are making me second guess myself. How could I have entertained the idea that I'd be able to drudge up the past?

June's presence erases the fleeting memory from my thoughts while her fully extended arm draws awareness to the discomfort the girl is forcing on me with her unrelenting questions. "That was quite the cough." She waggles the glass of water toward me. I nudge her outstretched hand away, annoyed that she has pinned me to the wall over George, and just as we were making strides.

At the mention of George's name, the whiskey hits the back of my throat, burning. I couldn't stop my reaction even if I wanted to. Whether it is the reintroduction of the drink after weeks of abstinence or the mention of the man who, at one time, I thought made the world turn. I can't be certain. If I am being honest, I'd rather not know. Either way, a coughing fit has me clutching at my throat while my face contorts in open-mouthed spasms.

My mind buzzes with too many thoughts, all of them rushing to seek words that will bring this assault on my emotions to a standstill.

I can't. No. I can't talk about that. There is not a day left upon this earth where I could speak about George in any way other than a lighthearted tale of the good old days. There is too much to lose. Never have I said the words out loud, avoidance being my steady companion all these years. The concerning thoughts that filter through my mind in the shape of nightmares have been easy enough to hold at bay in the bright of day. But on the heels of June's insistent questioning about the charges laid against me not making sense, I fear the truth that lies beneath a thin sheet of glass is in a precarious position of being shattered. The awareness of my inability to dole out the facts in small morsels paralyzes me to the core.

Writing off the worrisome notions as jumbled up, incorrect memories of actual events, I've done my best to remember George as the man I believed him to be. I force my resolve to stiffen once more though it takes every fiber of my being to do so. If this girl thinks she can convince me to say anything unbecoming of the man who held my heart in his hands, then she has another think coming.

My knee-jerk reaction to duck and cover takes over. I eye

June warily as she retakes her position on the sofa. The arguments for and against showing the girl to the door—and immediately ending any further discussion—ping-pong rapidly within the confines of my head.

Clearing my throat from the coughing incident, I gather myself up and regain my footing. The girl is looking at me expectantly, and it's all I can do to hold back the scoff that is ready to fly in her direction.

"Are you feeling better?" June asks, as though she hasn't just leveled me with her piercing inquisition.

"I'm fine." I am anything but fine, but she doesn't need to know that.

June smiles so sweetly I swear I can taste honey on my tongue. "Good. Shall we continue, then?"

I am as trapped as I've ever been. This was a bad idea. Allowing the girl into my home, the whiskey, the stories. All of it. What good did I think would come from digging up the past? My eyes dart around the room like a frightened rabbit trying to assess whether to flee or remain still. Maybe I can simply tell her a little about George, something that will satiate her quest for information, without revealing all my secrets.

I clear my throat again, willing my voice to deliver my words with strength instead of the rasping desperation of an old woman. I am ready to acquiesce, with my new plan of delivering tidbits of information at the forefront of my mind, when at the last minute, I lose my nerve. "I've changed my mind."

"What?" June's head snaps up, surprise emblazoned across her face.

"I don't think this is a good idea. People are going to believe what they want to believe, anyway." I try my hand at issuing an unconcerned appearance. "Besides, most folks around here have forgotten all about me and my story. There really isn't anything more to say on the matter."

"But—Meg. You can't be serious. I realize this is difficult for you, but—"

"But, nothing." I reinforce my words with an erect spine.

A weary sigh slips past the girl's lips. I assume she is disappointed, frustrated, maybe even a tad angry with my decision. I press my shoulders into the back of the chair, reinstating my determination.

June softens her demeanor along with her words. "You know, my grandmother used to tell me stories about her younger years. She was an ardent believer in a shared load being a lighter one. Her life was full and mostly enjoyable, yet she too experienced grievances and pain." The girl's shoulders lift and fall as if to say, *that's life*. "But the stories she told me, without fail, had two sides to them, just like the people she spoke of. What I learned is, not one person, not one story, not one experience, has only a single side."

June's head tilts to the right, and I presume she is scrutinizing my reaction. The girl continues, and I feel my resolve slipping.

"I imagine this is true when it comes to you—and also when it comes to George." June's expression begs for me to reconsider.

Catching myself from trusting too much, too soon, my hands grip the chair's armrests, seeking a sturdy object to ground myself with. "I am sorry this hasn't worked out, June." I reposition my hands, clasping them in my lap in an effort to pull any semblance of assuredness I have to the forefront. "But it is for the best."

"You're going to give up, then? Is that right?" June catches me off guard with the flash of anger that lines her question. I hadn't expected her to turn so quickly, but then again, I haven't given her much to go forward with.

I stiffen my posture assertively. "I don't look at it as giving up."

"Really? I find that strange. Since the formidable woman I met this afternoon didn't strike me as someone likely to back down from a fight." June's words challenge every ounce of my being.

June is more right than I imagine she realizes, but I must stop this at once. I was foolish to think dredging up the past was worth the risk. What if the eruption of the truth takes all of us down together? The girl can't possibly understand. She has no idea how what I have to say about my past could devastate her too.

Standing abruptly, I feel the full drive of my over-wrought emotions as they force me upright. Past my creaking hips and aching knees. Past my desire to maintain a semblance of decorum. Even past my hope of being able to alter the historical account of my life. "I don't want to disappoint you." The words bellow from my lips before I can reel them back in, and without a tick of the clock, I know I've said too much.

June's startled expression, lined with unspoken questions, and something I interpret as fear, sears itself into my mind. This isn't how I wanted the day to go. The girl must think I am right off my rocker. Sadly, I wouldn't blame her if she did.

My lungs burn, reminding me of the expiration date that was positioned over my head like a guillotine with the arrival of the doctor's letter. Time is running out on many things, and I am powerless to stop it.

I slump back into my chair, sending the pillow askew. Bent at the waist with my head in my hands, I mumble, "I don't want to disappoint anyone." The tears gather in my eyes, transforming my voice into stripped bare emotion. Though I fear the words and what they mean for me going forward, I force myself to say them, anyway. "I am better off remaining an outcast."

Sixteen

JUNE

THE FRUSTRATION THAT IS BREWING WITHIN ME over Meg's reluctance to speak of the past dulls in comparison as I witness the pain the woman is clearly experiencing in this moment. My eyes roam the room as I try to make sense of it all. Two house flies circle, going nowhere, in the small cyclone of air created by the fan oscillating in the corner of the living room.

Not unlike Meg and me.

I almost laugh at the irony, but my annoyance at our lack of progress holds the humor at bay.

My mind considers her words. Disappoint me? Why would it matter in the slightest to Meg whether or not I am disappointed by her? She doesn't know me from Adam. All I want is the story she promised me when we spoke on the phone, the interview she agreed to before I made the trek to Elko.

My fingers move to my head, first holding, then massaging. The pressure of a headache builds behind my eyes.

I am aware enough to understand Meg's turmoil is getting the best of her. Her past is something she had a hand in creating, and for that she must feel an immense amount of guilt. I feel for the woman, truly, I do. But if I don't convince her to reveal her story to me, I fear I'll never be viewed as a real reporter. Not by my editor, and certainly not by my father. Proving him wrong, I realize now, might have been an ill-advised motivation when deciding to journey to Elko.

My dreams of becoming the next Nellie Bly will be lost to the fanciful notions of a small child. I wasn't so arrogant to presume success would come easy, but if I am being honest; I didn't expect it requiring me to force an old woman into retelling a story that is certain to be riddled with remorse and embarrassment. All of it for the sake of advancing my career. My chin drops to my chest. This entire journey to Elko has been a fiasco. Defeat, shame, and disappointment battle for space within my heart.

Not being accustomed to wallowing, I immediately turn my thoughts on how to solve the problem before me. My job is to apply the skills I've learned as a reporter and coax Meg out of her refusal to speak with me. I sift through the lessons Harold Wilson, my editor, taught me in my first months as a reporter. One, be respectful of the other person's thoughts, feelings, and perspectives. Two, validate their experience with words and body language. Three, find common ground to connect over.

Tapping a finger to my bottom lip, I consider what Meg and I might have in common. At first glance, nothing comes to mind. She is decades older than me and, for that matter, Harold too. Maybe, his advice doesn't apply to every situation. If she doesn't want to talk, I am in no position to make her do so.

I give her another moment. I'll give her one more chance. If this doesn't prove fruitful, I will call it a day and leave this poor woman to her sad memories.

Meg releases a long exhale, and I read it as an invitation to engage. I circle back to an earlier topic, hoping for safer ground. "Meg, why were you no longer welcome at your parents' home?"

Silence is her only response.

"I see." My stomach grumbles its displeasure at not having been fed a proper meal in hours. I check my watch, noting the late hour will ensure a night spent at the local motel. If I'm being honest, I don't mind the extra hours of a night's sleep in Elko to contemplate what I will say to my father when I return home no further ahead than when I left in a hurry, anger fueling my departure. No one enjoys returning to the scene of an argument with their tail between their legs, but home, I concede, is where I must return to in the morning.

I've done all I can. An exasperated sigh sneaks through my closed lips. Reaching for my bag, I close my notebook and slide it, along with my pencil, inside.

Meg doesn't meet my eyes. She doesn't even look up as I stand. I push a bubble of irritation down while summoning a hefty dose of false professionalism. "Thank you for your time, Meg. I'll see myself out."

Turning one last time to consider the woman, I offer her a sincere smile. "I hope you find the peace you are seeking."

My hand is on the screen door latch when she calls out to me in a muted plea.

"Wait. Don't go."

I turn slowly to find Meg standing, somewhat haltingly, as she leans forward to pick up a glass of water from the tray on the coffee table.

"You think I'm just an old fool, dragging you all the way out here for no reason?" Her voice is ragged with emotion, rooting me to the floor.

I choose to remain tactful and offer nothing to confirm or deny the accuracy of her statement, but I show her I'm listening by removing my hand from the screen door's handle.

"Please." Meg gestures for me to sit again, her voice imploring me to do so.

I return to the sofa and take my seat again. Reaching for my recently abandoned glass of whiskey, I hope the strong drink will give me the boost I need to unearth a path forward. The woodsy scent of alcohol reaches my nose before the glass touches my lips.

The weight of my role in our standoff rests heavy on my shoulders. "I fear we've gotten off on the wrong foot."

Meg's red-rimmed eyes lift to meet mine as she settles herself once more in her chair. "How so?"

"I may not be the right reporter for you to confide in." A sheepish smile slips into place. "I thought if we worked together, we could write an article that we'd both be proud of. But I realize now I was only looking at things from my perspective. I hadn't considered yours, not truly, anyway. That doesn't make me well-suited to doing justice to your story. I was being selfish. For that, I am sorry."

I place the glass of whiskey back on the coffee table, my mis-step over pushing her too hard reflects back at me from Meg's watchful gaze. Knowing what I must do, I shift my hips against the lumpy sofa and prepare to stand once more.

"Please, June. Don't go."

A breath catches in my throat as my eyes find hers. With four paltry words, Meg's desperation shines a light on what I've been missing. She needs me as much as I need her. I was right to think this was something we could only accomplish by working together.

I weigh the options before me. There is no guarantee here. I may waste time and still come up empty. A front-page article with my name on the byline remains my goal, but somehow, in this moment, with Meg's beaten down anguish on full display, it seems less important now. Meg may very well continue to stare daggers at me or shout profanities and resist my questions, but then again, she might open up and share the truth that has yet to see the light of day. I have no way of explaining the sensation burning deep within me. I only know my desire to understand the events of Meg's life feels essential to my own, and I'm unable to ignore my instincts, regardless of my inability to understand them.

"Thank you for staying." Meg's voice is full of rasp as it breaks into my ruminating mind.

I offer a slight nod before running my fingers through my hair. I tuck swaths of blonde strands behind my ears as I come to terms with the situation before us.

Like it or not, Meg's and my boats are tied together in choppy waters. She needs me to obtain the redemption I can only assume she is eager to embrace, and I need her to secure advancement in my career. Not unlike Meg, I've been desperate too. Desperate to prove myself as a reporter and a woman.

This is what connects us. As if someone has turned the lights on inside my head, I see it clearly now. Meg said it herself, "They assumed their thoughts and ideas were the only ones and there was little room for discussion when I had something to contribute." She was speaking of the men she worked alongside in the bootleg operation.

It occurs to me that in thirty years, little has changed for women. Sure, we have decades of accomplishments behind us, including securing the vote, replacing men in the workplace during the war, and more. But what we don't have is equality. Not in the true sense of the word, that is.

Our work is undervalued, monetarily and otherwise. Credit for a job well-done, like in the case of my front-page article, is stripped from us and then peddled as being something to protect us from harm. If we had equality, I consider for the first time, women wouldn't be in harm's way for succeeding in their chosen careers. Our voices being suppressed is what I fear most. A woman's perspective may not be a mirror image of a man's, but that, I believe, is exactly the point. Men and women both have value to offer in important conversations. A woman's voice is needed, if only to provide a fresh perspective. Whether it is around the dinner table, the water cooler, or the boardroom, a woman's voice is an asset.

Watching Meg, I see in her the push and pull of wanting to speak her truth while the fear of being shamed for it does its best to convince her otherwise. Too often, women haven't been taken at their word. This is something I can work with.

With a fire in my belly, the path before me is clear. I am far more interested in helping the woman unburden herself from decades of pain, self-loathing, and silence. The realization that I may not get the notoriety I came here seeking by writing this article pokes at me from behind, but I lift my chin with an unwavering determination I've seldom known in my role as a reporter.

Meg is worth the risk. Because if I succeed in telling Meg's story, we all take another step closer to lifting our voices.

Sitting with my hands clasped lightly in my lap, I offer Meg an encouraging smile. "Whenever you are ready. Please, take your time. There is no need to rush."

Meg turns her water glass with a nervous twitch between both hands. Her unease over what she is willing herself to commit to echoes in the steady squeak of glass against damp palms.

Recognizing her anguish, I want to put her at ease. "We have a common goal, you and I. Do you agree?"

Meg looks at me, a question lining her expression.

I am not inclined to let Meg Bruno walk all over me when I feel certain that we can accomplish so much more by working together. However, I must show her she can trust me. That is at the heart of the solution before us.

"I have no intention of pushing you if you do not wish to be pressed on the matter. You invited me into your life and your home in the capacity of my being a reporter. My job is to get to the heart of the story. I have people to answer to in Carson City, Meg. But..." I hesitate, wanting my words to be enough to convince her I mean her no harm. "We need to trust one another if we're both to arrive at a favorable outcome. You, I presume, want to tell your side of the events that took place in January, 1926. I want to record and share those events with a wider audience."

Meg nods her head once, and I take it as a sign that she understands.

I pick up my glass of whiskey and take a warming sip. My relief at having found a path forward with Meg is tucked well out of sight, behind a manufactured mask of put upon composure. I incline my head and encourage her as gently as I can with a heart full of compassion and a willingness to listen to all that she has to tell me.

"Don't you want to get your notebook out?" Meg's eyes land on the bag at my feet.

I shake my head. "I'd much rather listen. You have my full attention, Meg."

Seventeen

MEG

I place my empty glass on the small table beside my chair. I've not been fair to the girl. Wasting her afternoon with my bullheadedness, I'll admit, has not been one of my finer moments, and I've had more than a few of those over the years.

"My parents died thinking I was a disappointment." I feel the weight of my shame as it threatens to engulf me. I breathe the words out in a whisper. "This is what I regret most."

My eyes shift up to June's, and I am thankful to find a concerned expression shaping her features.

Memories of home wash over me, twitching my lips upward. "I grew up on a vineyard. In Napa Valley. I loved living in Napa. Vineyards and grape growers surrounded us on all sides. Delicious food, an abundance of wine, and plenty of people to share it with." I beam, as the years, long gone now, filter through my mind. "I was at home there."

My eyes survey the room, transforming my delighted expression into a scowl. The well-worn sofa, the drab walls in need of a fresh coat of paint. Even the mismatched furniture seems to long for happier times. That is what they were, on the vineyard. Simple but happier, all the same.

June shifts her position on the sofa, crossing one leg over the other. "Why were you no longer welcomed? At home, I mean."

Though I suspect she may have guessed the answer, I indulge her question anyway. "Money got tight when the Volstead Act came into existence. Like all vineyards, what was once our livelihood became an illegal existence with the flipping of a calendar year. But it was more complicated than that. Grape farmers lost their vineyards, their homes, and more if they weren't able or were unwilling to adapt to the changing times. Some plowed under the vines, planting crops of walnuts or plums, but you must understand, it takes years for trees to produce, not to mention, earn."

June's head bobs with consideration.

"When the law finally allowed church leaders to help manage vineyards that were granted sacramental wine permits, my father's winery was one of the fortunate ones. At least I thought us fortunate in the beginning."

The view beyond the window is dark, drawing my attention. The sun, now set, has surely left its scorch on the Nevada desert, and I imagine it will be hours before the house is cool enough to embrace a comfortable sleep.

"What happened?" June leans forward, placing an elbow on top of her crossed knee.

"Do you have any siblings, June?" Though I already know the girl is an only child, I am keen to explain the depth and forgiving nature of a sibling relationship. She may not understand the bond that for most of my life has been an unbreakable one, but I feel I must try to make her comprehend such a thing. If she is unable to do so, she will never make sense of my reasons for doing what I did.

"No. I have no siblings. My mother..." June's eyes glisten with a hint of moisture in the lamplight. "She had several miscarriages."

I suck in a sharp breath. I knew the girl was an only child, but I had considered little beyond that. Being made aware of her mother's heartache though, I wasn't prepared for that. Before June can finish her thought, the despair I know too well as my own creeps toward me.

"She struggled in the early years with pregnancies. She likes to tell me I am the gift she was to wait patiently for. I suspect it is her way of finding the light within the storm."

"I am sorry for her losses." The words stammer, above a whisper, past my lips. The grief that accompanies the toll of a failed pregnancy is something I understand all too well. I have thought often of how my life might have turned out had a child been born. Pushing the torment from my mind, I continue. "I have an older brother."

"You mentioned him earlier."

"He was the kind of older brother who made me feel special, like ours was a bond that no one could come between. It was the two of us against the world, or at the very least, our parents, if we'd found ourselves in a spot of trouble."

I chuckle as a movie reel of memories plays across my mind. An image of Matteo and me in our parents' bedroom comes to mind. He was twelve and knew better but I was six and happy to follow my big brother wherever he roamed. His face shone with mischief and determination when he convinced me to try on Mother's Sunday bonnet while he affixed Father's tie around his neck. We must have spent the entire afternoon dressing up and playing the role of debonair society people while our parents, busy in the vineyard, were none the wiser.

Matteo was always looking to have better than our happy, but far from opulent, lot in life. The smile slips from my lips as I contemplate the early signs of Matteo's quest for more as they become sharper in my mind's eye. By the time we were discovered, Father's tie was mangled beyond repair and Mother's lipstick was smeared across my cheeks, her dressing table, and the quilt placed at the foot of their bed. Matteo got a whooping and I, being the younger and more impressionable child, got a good scrubbing before we were both sent to bed without dinner.

My poor parents.

I lift my gaze to meet June's. I push down my unease at having caused my family such grief and clear my throat. "He had a knack for making me feel significant. So much so that he could also talk me into doing things, pranks and such. All of them, sure to get me in trouble."

"Ah, he was a prankster," June teases, and I am silently thankful for her attempt at lightening the mood in the room.

"He was." I temper my words, worry over how they will sound when spoken aloud holding me back. "But he was also a dreamer. He wanted more than the simple life of a grape farmer."

"I imagine his dreams caused some family discord." June fills in the blanks with her comment.

"You could say that." I am at a crossroads. Telling June means risking her opinion of me. I shouldn't care what the girl thinks of me, but I know now, after all these years, that I was the weak one. The one who didn't stand up for what was right. I am not proud of my actions, and in that sense, I was as much at fault as Matteo had been for bringing shame on our family.

If only he hadn't demanded my involvement in his scheme, I would have lived out my life on the vineyard, tending the vines in ignorant bliss. I release a slow exhale. "Sorry. I am aware you'll need to know this to understand everything that happened after, but I'm not sure how to say the words." A despondent sigh follows close on the heels of my apology.

June's expression turns serious. "I am not here to judge you, Meg. I'm here to listen. If you ask me, knowing you have regrets tells me more about the person you've become since then."

Grasping June's vote of encouragement like it's the last sliver of hope, I shove all propriety aside and speak in a rush. "My brother struck a deal with the church manager of our vineyard. He bought back my father's sacramental wine and sold it on the black market for the entirety of Prohibition."

"That's where the wine that was seized came from." June's face dawns with understanding. "All eight hundred and twenty gallons of it."

Deciding not to answer her question outright, I do what I can to explain further. "I was roped into his plans because my brother lived in Elko and needed someone he could trust to transport the wine in Napa from the church's storage facility to a secret location. From there, he arranged to have someone else pick up the wine without the risk of being found out. He cajoled me with promises of financial security for our family, along with assurances that a woman would never be caught moving crates of wine. At the time, I assumed he meant by anyone, but now I know he only meant by the authorities. He was my older brother, so I took him at his word, despite my initial trepidation."

My chin drops to my chest in shame as tears gather in my eyes. "I'll never forget the day my parents discovered what I was doing. It was July, 1922 when my father arrived at the church's warehouse unexpectedly one afternoon, probably looking to speak with the manager about the upcoming harvest. I'd been bootlegging for my brother for less than a month, and I was still getting used to the routine. My attention was focused on loading up my father's farm truck, tucking blankets from my mother's linen cupboard around crates of Brunelli Vineyard sacramental labeled wine when he came across me at the back of the flung open warehouse doors."

June doesn't utter a word, but I swear I can sense the gasp she is holding back, in what I assume is for my benefit.

"His face flared red. I'd never seen him so angry, all of it directed toward me. I tried to explain. Tried to tell him I was earning money for the family, but he wouldn't hear a word of it."

A sigh laced with decades-old guilt leaks from within me. "By the time I had hurried home after dropping the load at Matteo's designated location, I was desperate to explain myself. But when I arrived back at the vineyard." My head shakes of its own volition. "My belongings had been hastily packed and were waiting for me on the front porch. He demanded I leave the family home at once. My mother stood there, watching through the kitchen window with tears rolling down her cheeks."

The words break as they croak from my lips. "I never got to say goodbye."

"Oh, Meg. I'm so sorry." June coos despite hearing my confession that I was not only breaking my parents' hearts, I was also breaking the law.

My head jerks back and forth at the grief running through me. "I left for Elko that same day. My father died a few months later." An anguished sob erupts without warning. "My mother, the following year."

Tears stream toward the floor, routing around the crevices of wrinkles and the sorrow embedded upon my face. "So, you see, my parents died knowing I was a disappointment. What I did..." The words stutter out of me in between sobs. "They died of broken hearts and I was the one who did the breaking."

Several minutes pass with the only sound being the sobbing I'm struggling to gain control over. Besides my brother, I have told no one how or why I came to live in Elko. I find myself rattled by the realization that I actually managed to do so in the girl's presence, but here we are, left to process the gravity of it all.

I sneak a glance in June's direction, trying to gauge where her thoughts lie. She could just as easily walk out my door, branding me with the harsh words I am more than deserving of. I wouldn't fault her if she did. If I'm being honest, I might even welcome the rebuke.

My tears quieten to the occasional sniffle as the wave of emotion subsides.

"Thank you for telling me. You were brave to do so."

June stands and passes me a tissue she's pulled from her bag. "I'm sure it wasn't easy."

I take the offered tissue and wipe my nose.

"I have one question, though." June takes her seat as she considers her next words.

I look at the girl, well aware I am in the soup now and the only way out is to go through, no matter how difficult it may be. "Only one?" My attempt to make light of her comment garners me a faint smile.

"Did your parents know about your brother's involvement? With the bootlegged wine?"

"No. I never had the chance to explain fully. My father wouldn't hear anything I had to say. He simply showed me the door."

I marvel at the girl's mind. Her ability to find the thread I imagine others would leave unconsidered. Matteo always seems to come out on top. No matter how dire the situation, others view him as being able to do no wrong. This time, I am grateful for June's observation. She has showed her awareness that there is more to the story than meets the eye. Though I was slow to learn to distrust my brother, June has insight beyond her years.

I am wiping the damp from my eyes when she asks. "What happened to the Brunelli vineyard, after your parents passed?"

A tortured laugh bursts from my chest. "My brother inherited everything. The vineyard, the farmhouse, and the sacramental wine permit. As far as I know, he kept the vineyard, at least until Prohibition ended in 1933."

June's eyebrows lift high on her forehead, and I know in an instant—the girl is someone I can trust. I raise my gaze to June's, bolstered by her reaction to what I've said thus far. A subtle stirring of butterflies in my stomach matches the intentions swirling inside my head. I will tell the girl about my time in jail and see how that goes. But first, I look down at my wrinkled and tired looking day dress. I must clean myself up. "I'll be right back. I want to freshen up a bit."

Eighteen

JUNE

MEG EXCUSES HERSELF, LEAVING ME TO PONDER all she's said. My fingers itch to make notes, but I resist the urge, putting Meg's trust in me over my need to capture every detail in writing. A finger taps my bottom lip as I attempt to piece the details together.

Meg's brother, Matteo, was the name she mentioned. His presence in her life pokes at the edges of my mind, and not in a good way. I can't help but wonder how embroiled he was in the bootleg operation that landed her in jail. What if Meg is protecting her brother from his involvement in the raid? All these years later, would she do such a thing? I search my memory. There was no mention of a Matteo Brunelli in any of the archived articles, I'm certain of it. A shared last name among the newspapers and court records would have been a dead giveaway of the family connection. That is not a detail I would have overlooked.

I stand and move toward the small space in front of the

window, its view to the outside obscured by a half-closed curtain and a pitch black night. I notice, for the first time, the stifling heat from earlier in the afternoon is finally relenting, if only by a fraction of a degree closer to the window.

Giving credence to the awareness that I often think better while in motion, I follow a path, back and forth across the room, encouraging the mountain of jumbled thoughts that are confounding me to bubble up to the surface so I can snatch them into my awareness.

"Wait!" I say to the empty room, pausing mid-stride as I recall Meg's words. She took a page out of her brother's book when deciding to change her name. Matteo must have changed his name before Meg ever thought to do so herself, but when and to what?

Perhaps he was also arrested. I rifle through my mind for the names of the eight arrested and charged that January in 1926, but there isn't a single name that comes close to resembling a shortened version of Matteo.

Even though Meg hasn't uttered a disparaging word against him, something tells me her brother may have been shifty enough to avoid getting caught altogether. With the handful of insights Meg shared with me, my gut tells me not to trust her brother or his involvement in the raid, but I have nothing concrete to back up my suspicions.

I will have to wait to hear what Meg has to say on the topic, though I suspect she may not be inclined to share more if she is indeed protecting her only sibling. Either way, I feel as though I've been given a jigsaw puzzle with missing pieces, and no amount of thinking about the problem by myself will fill in the blank spaces. I need Meg's help to complete this picture.

Though I have no concrete evidence to warrant such an

opinion, I feel my hackles rise when I think of Matteo benefitting while Meg suffered. First by not being found out by his parents, and second, by inheriting the vineyard after their deaths. Add to that, the knowledge he continued to profit from the vineyard's black market activities all the way through to 1933, when Prohibition ended. A full decade after the passing of their parents.

As a reporter, I am well aware I shouldn't be choosing sides, especially when there are too many details missing to comprehend the situation in full. Right or wrong, as a young woman who is still reeling from a ridiculous argument with my father over what is best for my life, I am certain my personal feelings on having a man dictate my future have pushed their way into my interpretation of Meg's experience. I am probably overreacting, but in the past several months the tension that lies between my father and me has given me reason to doubt my abilities as a reporter. My intense desire to spread my wings has been matched by his determination to clip them.

Touching the pearls at my neck, I straighten my posture and remind myself of the job at hand. It is the story, the truth history has buried, that I am here to obtain. Yet I feel a sense of duty to Meg. Despite her giving me little reason to side with her, I am beginning to see glimpses of the frightened woman beneath the facade.

My thoughts turn to the Brunelli vineyard. I wonder if it still exists. Meg didn't confirm it outright, but a hunch tells me the wine from the 1926 raid came from her family vineyard, but what about now? Is there a piece of Meg's past still thriving and earning in Napa Valley? I make a mental note to do more digging for the vineyard when I return to Carson City. But first I'll need to acquire further details from Meg.

I hear her shuffling down the hall before she enters the room, face washed clean of tears with only a few splotches of red puffiness to tell the tale of her recent emotions. She has changed into a billowing house dress, it's blue-green, collared, button-up highlighted by large yellow daisies adorning both oversized front pockets. The lack of a fashionable cinched waist makes the frail woman appear swallowed up by the fabric, though I keep my thoughts on her state of dress to myself.

"Feeling better?" I infuse my words with what I hope is a concerned tone, noting that despite the still warm living room, the woman has once again pulled a sweater on over top of her dress.

"A little." Her sheepish response tells me we must be making progress, and I breathe a sigh of relief that I've not been met with yet another piercing comment. "My mother always said a change of clothes is as pleasing as a change of mood."

Taking my seat on the sofa, I decide it's better not to hesitate and instead jump right back in. "I am curious about Matteo."

I see Meg stiffen out of the corner of my eye, and I immediately question my insight on the progress I assumed we were making. Deciding it is better to ask for forgiveness rather than permission, I hide my awareness at her renewed discomfort, and I press forward. "What was his involvement in the bootlegging business back in 1926?"

Meg doesn't move to sit. Instead, her hands find each other and twist together in what I can only guess is worry.

I try again to coax her out, despite knowing the answer to my next question. "He was still involved in bootlegging Brunelli Vineyard wine, wasn't he?"

Meg sucks in a sharp breath, bumping her back into the wall that separates the kitchen from the living room. I cock my head to one side, trying to understand where her fresh reluctance is coming from. The idiom, one step forward, two steps back, comes to mind as I watch the woman's reaction.

My fatigue from the day is creeping in, lowering my resistance to the mounting frustration thrumming through my veins. "I only ask because you mentioned he inherited the vineyard after your parents' passing, so I assume, since it was wine that was seized during the raids, that the Brunelli vineyard was still in play in 1926."

Meg is giving me all indications that I've once again touched a nerve, but I don't know if there is a better approach for this conversation. Ten minutes ago, she shared heartbreaking details about her family life and now she appears to be clamming up. It's hard to ignore the nagging thoughts about her brother. I am right to think Matteo is at the heart of something Meg is holding back from me.

At first, I assumed it was an unbreakable sibling connection, just as Meg herself had indicated, but now, with Meg dancing around my mention of Matteo's involvement in the bootlegging operation and more importantly the raid itself, I am wondering if there is something more nefarious at play.

"Why don't we move out to the porch?" Meg's invitation croaks free of her wrinkled throat. "I imagine the night air is cooler now."

"Okay. But Meg, you'll eventually have to tell me more about your brother's involvement. If he was involved at all." The fierce look in her eyes reveals her lack of inclination to do so. She must have realized that she said too much and now she is once again desperate to back-pedal.

I watch in surprise as the woman coerces her body into straightening as tall as she is able. I imagine a rod of steel lining her spine in an effort to dodge my questions. "When it comes to my brother, I think I've said enough for now. Come." Meg's voice softens a touch. "Fresh air will do us both some good. Then I'll tell you about my time in jail." She gestures to the front door with an outstretched hand.

Nineteen

MEG

THE COOL NIGHT SKY IS A WELCOME REPRIEVE, reinvigorating my senses after an emotional afternoon. I make a trip back to the kitchen before placing two glasses of water on the round metal table. The weight of the glasses causes the uneven table legs, speckled with rust, to slant to one side with a light thud against the wood of the narrow porch's floor boards.

June carries a kitchen chair through the screen door while I slide the rocker over to make room beside the table. A quick scan of the chair, its blue vinyl cracking in places, spurs me to claim it as my own.

"I'll take the kitchen chair. Here. You sit on the rocker." I step aside to allow the girl to pass. My hands clasp together, wringing with apprehension as to what could possibly come next. "I apologize for my lack of hospitality." Feeling the heat of a blush creep up my neck, I take another step away from the shadowy brightness of the light reaching the porch from inside the house. Thankful I can hide my shame under the cover of darkness, I try to explain further. "I'm not used to entertaining guests."

"You have nothing to apologize for. Besides, I am not here for you to entertain." Though I am certain the girl means it in a polite, non-obligatory way, I feel the sharp end of her professional motivations for being here and wonder if a reporter is capable of stepping out from under the umbrella of their job.

June inhales, sucking in the cool air. "You were right. The night air feels good." She gestures toward me. "Aren't you warm with the sweater?"

I take a seat, shifting my hips against the hard vinyl. "I prefer to be warm." My plain response isn't inaccurate as it stands, but it is far from complete, and also another topic I prefer not to delve into. Some things are simply not easily shareable.

June's face lights up. "I just remembered. I'll be right back."

Jumping up from the rocker like only a twenty-three-year-old can do, she bounds down the three porch steps and jogs toward the station wagon parked a few feet away in the gravel driveway. I watch the girl as her torso disappears into the backseat of what I presume is her parents' station wagon. Popping back out, she closes the car door and jogs back toward me with a round green Tupperware container in hand.

"I forgot I had these." June raises the container like a trophy above her head as she climbs the steps. "Mom's chocolate chip and oatmeal cookies are the best."

Removing the lid, June offers the cookies toward me. I peer into the container. The scent of fresh-baked cookies, warm from a day of resting in the car, rises to greet me. I pull a single cookie free, noting that June's mom must have sent her to Elko with an entire batch of cookies. An image of June living an idyllic childhood forms in my mind's eye, and I long to have witnessed such an experience. Either way, I am pleased by the thought of what clearly was a happy childhood for the girl.

"Thank you." I say before biting into the moist and deliciously sweet home-baked treat.

"Good. Right?" June smiles before biting into her own cookie.

"Very good. Please give your mother my thanks." I examine the cookie in the shadowy light. A stab of nostalgia pierces my armor. "I haven't had fresh-baked cookies since I lived at the vineyard."

"You don't bake? Not even for yourself?" I can feel the girl's despair at not having the luxury of something that must be a staple in her life.

I shake my head and savor the last bite of cookie.

June places the container in the center of the rickety table. "Have as many as you like. I'm not sure I could live without home-baked cookies."

"It's amazing what one can live without." The silence grows between us as I contemplate all that I've lost through the years. There are the obvious things like my family, my home, my place in the Napa Valley community. Even during my time in jail, I lived without my freedom, among other niceties of life. But what pains me the most is the knowledge that I've lived without my own sense of self for far longer than I'd care to admit.

I assume the girl senses my need for contemplation, so we munch in silence, save for the hum of nearby cicadas. We devour three more cookies each before I get the sense that June is biding her time, waiting for me to resume where I left off. I brush my hands against one another, ready to begin.

"I was released from jail on a Tuesday." I cannot see beyond the porch railing, but my gaze lingers past the recognizable into the darkness. "It was late May. The day was warm, which to me was a welcome reprieve from the damp of the cement block cell. I've never been as cold as I was in those months in jail." I wrap my sweater tighter around my middle, smothering the beginning of a shiver that is ready to elicit chill bumps down my arms, before wrenching my attention away from the memory altogether.

June pushes her saddle-shoe clad foot into the floorboard, setting the rocker in motion. The familiar squeak-swoosh of the chair's route comforts me, lulling me into contemplation.

"The timeline of events." June's voice is soft. "I meant to ask you about the sentence versus the time you spent in jail. They don't add up and I wondered why?"

"Ah, the shortened sentence?" I let out a slow exhale and see June's head swaying with the rocker's motion in my periphery.

"I was arrested on January 12th. By mid-February, I had been charged with eleven counts of selling liquor to minors."

"Yes." The girl draws the word out. "I'm aware." June's voice is threaded with irritation, which I assume is due to the time it takes me to deliver that which she seeks. Though I suspect she is attempting to keep her frustration under wraps, it pokes at me anyway. "Meg, I've seen the court records."

My back goes up in resistance to her third-party insight, turning the sweet remnants of the cookie into something far more bitter. "I thought you wanted me to tell you my story. I am trying to do that."

The girl's annoyance oozes out of her in the shape of a huff as her body connects with the hard back of the rocking chair. A non-verbal *fine* is my translation of her movements.

"There was a quick trial in March, which you are well aware of. I pled guilty to all eleven charges against me. Then the judge issued a $750 fine and sentenced me to a three-hundred-and-ninety-day jail term. Ninety days for the first charge and thirty days for each subsequent charge. It was all very proper and legal. I had already been in jail for more than sixty days while awaiting trial and those days counted toward my sentence."

"Yes, but you only served one hundred and twenty-eight days. That is my question. Why were you released early?"

"Maybe I was a model prisoner. Did you consider that?" I shoot back, sarcasm lacing my words. "Only served one hundred and twenty-eight days. Have you ever been imprisoned for a single day in all your life? I think not." The words huff out of me in a jumble of murmured annoyances. Weary from the day's events and the girl's continual probing, I have resorted once again to childish responses. I am helpless to stop, and instead refuse to answer any more questions on principle alone.

Twenty

JUNE

The porch rocker continues its song of swoosh, squeak, with the occasional light thud coming from the sound of my shoe tapping the wood floorboards as I push off. Determined to maintain the rocker's calming effect on me, I sip from my glass of water while doing everything I can to wait Meg out.

How the conversation between us spirals downward so fast, I have no idea. All I can assume is, her pain is not a distant memory despite the almost thirty years that have passed. Instead, her regrets torment her like a cancer lying just beneath the surface of Meg's skin. Ready to assert itself in an angry rage at a moment's notice or, in my case, at a question deemed impertinent by Meg.

There is a feistiness to her that I have to admit I admire, even if she continues to intimidate me regularly. Either way, I am not inclined to let her know this since I have yet to pry the truth of what took place all those years ago out of her clenched fists.

My mother, a former doctor's office receptionist, used to tell me that pain is far more difficult to deal with when a person is tense. Whether it was a scraped knee or the tonsillectomy I had as a child, her advice was always the same.

Breathe, June. Breathe through the pain and the pain will become easier to bear.

I consider her words now and wonder if the same advice applies to the pain of an anguished heart.

Minutes pass as we sit, each of us resolute in our standing and our silence. I contemplate all the things I don't have answers to, stealing the occasional glance in Meg's direction every few minutes to gauge her mood.

The air between us shifts when a light breeze whispers up the porch steps, washing over us as it slips through the mesh of the screen door and into the house beyond. I imagine the wind coaxing me with its lightness to set my pride aside and see if we can move past our silent standoff.

Aware I am unlikely to receive an answer to my question of why Meg was released early from jail, I try another approach to get her talking again. "When you were released from jail, what did you do then?"

Meg's gaze slides over to mine, examining me as if I've lost my marbles or perhaps only my memory. "I told you, I returned to my apartment."

"Yes." I push down the exasperated sigh that is ready to fly. "I remember you mentioning the return to your apartment and the realization that the federal Prohibition agents must not have initially suspected you nor your place as being involved with the others arrested since they didn't search the speakeasy or your apartment."

A firm nod of her head is the only reply. I allow several more minutes to pass before deciding to try again. Accepting her non-verbal confirmation is likely the only answer she is going to grant me.

"Well, I am happy to talk more about the federal agents, their lack of suspicion, and the outcome of your sentence if you like, but what I meant was, what did you do after returning from your time spent in jail?"

Her voice is hoarse, the gruffness reminding me to tread carefully. "I couldn't very well go back to the warehouse and the life of a bootlegger." A shrug of her shoulders gives me little to go on. "I just gathered myself together, tried to sort out what to do next."

I've got her talking again. A small tingle of triumph rises within me as I try to imagine Meg returning to her apartment after being released from jail.

"Okay." I draw out the word as my brain works to find another avenue in which to gain access to the information I need to create some semblance of a news article.

"Let's start with this, then." I brighten at the thought of approaching the questions from a new, and hopefully less confrontational, angle. "When did you come to live here? In this house?"

Meg must deem my question suitable as she doesn't hesitate to answer.

"Oh, I've been here for years. Moved into the place in 1927. Yes, it was February, 1927."

Recognition at what I am getting at dawns as a sheepish lift of her shoulders offers what I choose to interpret as an apology of sorts. "I stayed at the apartment for another eight months before relocating." Her voice dwindles into a murmur. "My time there is a blur. It was all a bit much to take in, you see."

"What was?" I reach for another cookie and bite into it, hoping my appearing distracted will aid Meg's ability to confide in me without the pressure of my inquiring eyes peering at her.

"I didn't speak to anyone, you know, from before." A dejected sigh escapes her pursed lips. "The day I was taken into custody was the same day I found myself ostracized from the only friends I had."

My heart lurches at the thought of Meg being abandoned by the so-called friends of her bootlegging operation, yet my mind leaps to ask whether her brother is included with that lot. "What do you mean?"

"How was I to know if the feds were following me, hoping to nab the others? It was a risk none of us could take." Another shrug of her shoulders tells me she isn't entirely okay with this outcome. "Protect the tribe and then protect the merchandise."

"What?" My head swivels with speed in Meg's direction.

"George always said, the first rule of being a bootlegger is above all else, you protect the tribe."

"So, none of the men were arrested with you? None of them involved in the business?" I tilt my head in question. The incredulity of this information feels like a punch to the stomach. "You never spoke to them again? How can that be? From the little you've told me, you were all thick as..." My words trail off as I realize my choice of words may not be well received given the topic of our conversation.

"I never spoke to them again. A note was shoved under my apartment door in the dead of night two days after I was released from jail. The note, written in an unfamiliar hand, instructed me to steer clear of anything and everyone from my life before. I had my bootlegging earnings and some money from the speakeasy's profits stashed. I owned the building outright having paid cash with the money I'd earned those first five months on the job. George had gifted me a few jewels over the years too, so I knew I could follow instructions and wait it out. I restocked my cupboards with groceries, got enough supplies to sustain me for a week or two, and I holed myself up in the apartment and waited."

"So, you were expecting someone to reach out then?" I feel the weight of Meg's loss as if it is emanating off her in sheets of heat like a noon-day sun against a freshly paved Nevada highway.

"I was." Meg drains her glass of water. "After a month of waiting with no contact being received, I decided it was time to put the past behind me and move forward. I came around to the realization that I wasn't going to get the answers to the questions I had. I certainly wasn't eager to re-enter the bootlegging business. Not since I'd been identified as a felon. The risk was too great for everyone involved. So, I spent another month or two cleaning up all evidence of the speakeasy and preparing to sell the building."

The rocker pitches forward, squealing in protest as my weight shifts in it. "Wait. Meg, you had questions too?"

Meg inclines her head but offers nothing more. We sit in silence, each of us ruminating on our shared but unspoken contemplations. My brain turns jumbled thoughts over and over until an idea pokes through the tangle of uncertainties.

Whether Meg knows it or not, she is the key to understanding everything. She may think she doesn't know what truly transpired in 1926, but my gut tells me otherwise. Coming to terms with what she knows is the challenge before us. As far as I can tell, it is the only path forward if she is to get to the heart of why she was the sole individual to go to jail.

"That must have been difficult, being alone, not knowing where your friends were or what you were expected to do next. Especially after being such a close-knit group, like I am guessing you were." Meg lifts her head, a pained expression stretching her lips into a thin line. "You were brave to go it alone." I emphasize the word brave, hoping she will hear me and take the title as her own.

I watch as her shoulders settle and her back straightens. "I had little choice then. All I could do was what I needed to do in order to survive."

My words are doing as I hoped they would, infusing her with the recognition she has likely never received at having towed her own road, by herself, all these years. Even in 1955, women are frowned upon if they remain unmarried, choosing alternate paths through life. I can't imagine the daily struggles Meg faced in 1927. "Yet, you persevered. That is something to be proud of."

Meg's tone is flat, all emotion from the long day and difficult conversation making itself known. "Courage is seldom summoned under comfortable circumstances, June. I only wish I had been courageous much earlier in my life. Then, perhaps, I wouldn't have lived such a lonely existence."

I open my mouth, searching for an appropriate response but am stopped short as I take in Meg's features in the dim light. She sits before me, a woman broken from the weight of a life filled with regret.

Twenty-One

MEG

I FEEL THE GIRL'S GAZE ON ME AND SHAKE MYSELF free from the rare moment of pity. Speaking of such things docs me little good, and I've no one to blame but myself. The choice is simple, if not easy: I can either continue to wallow in what once was or make amends and move forward. All I need now is the strength to do so.

In a quick glance, I catch June's youthful eagerness mixed with a depth of compassion I've seldom had shone in my direction, and I feel my heart squeeze. I only wish there was a guarantee to things turning out alright in the end.

Before she can barrage me with more questions, I head her off. "Anyway, I sold the building and upstairs apartment for a decent amount, purchased this place and tucked the rest away to live off." My hand waves toward the house at our backs. "I know it could use some work. The extreme weather isn't kind to much around these parts and now with most of the money spent, the government pension only stretches so far."

I try to edge the sadness from my smile. "It's not the high life, but I've got more than many, so I am fortunate enough."

June's lips quirk into a bemused grin. "Did you experience much of a high life? During Prohibition, I mean."

A chuckle releases as though my body is accustomed to handing laughter out regularly. Perhaps the girl is rubbing off on me, after all. "Some. It wasn't often, given the amount of work involved with the bootlegging life, but there were moments of gaiety."

"Tell me about the high life, Meg."

My head lolls back, granting happier times of the past access to play across my memory. If I squint my eyes just so, I can make out the memory of a holiday season in the twinkle of the stars hanging above us in the indigo night sky.

I steal a sideways glance in June's direction. "The night we opened Bootlegger's Bluff was certainly something to remember."

June leans forward, placing her elbows on top of her knees, bringing the rocker to a silent standstill.

"Though most folks just called it The Bluff, my little speakeasy was the place to be. It was the newest joint in Elko in December 1922 and the opening was primed perfectly for the jubilant timing of the holiday season."

I feel butterflies in my stomach as the memory of opening night washes over me.

"I was nervous at first, not wanting to draw attention to myself or the rest of the bootleg operation, but George was insistent The Bluff was a prime opportunity to secure my financial future."

My lips twist as I think back to how my unmarried status became a financial boon, despite my reluctance to remain single. "As a femme sole, I was able to purchase property and run a business under my own name. My life running booze from California to Elko was already busy and came with enough risk and illegal activity, so to say I was hesitant about the idea is an understatement."

I feel the hint of a blush as it warms my cheeks. "He finally convinced me when he whispered in his sultry Italian accent, *Amore mio, my love, I want to know that you will be taken care of if anything should ever happen to me.* Until that moment, I had never had anyone want to protect me in such a way. I had never before felt so loved."

My hand reaches for my empty water glass, rotating its bottom with rhythmic twists against the top of the small table as I try to disguise my embarrassment at such an intimate memory.

June's head bobs in understanding. "I imagine he was quite convincing."

"That he was." I tuck a self-conscious smile out of sight as the memory of George's words comes to life inside my mind.

Drawing June's attention back to The Bluff and away from George, I feel a thrill of excitement as I remember how I loved the space I created for my business venture. "Beautiful glass bottles in a variety of colors lined a shelf against the back wall behind the bar."

I wave my hand in the air, seeing the glimmer in my mind's eye. "You should have seen how the light sparkled around the room, sending a rainbow of colors whenever the candlelight hit just right."

My hand comes down and slaps my lap with an excited

thwap. "There was a gleaming plank of black oak polished to a shine that served as the bar with several fabric-covered bar stools lining up like soldiers in front of it."

"The room was intimate and almost magical." I feel a shudder of glee course through me. "When it snowed that winter, the coziness of the place seemed to grow in spades. We had clusters of little round tables and chairs throughout and our drinks were poured into real glasses. We even hid our diluting tubs of water under the tables, then covered the tables with linens."

A contemplative finger taps my bottom lip. "The tubs were something we never had to use, thank heavens, but had we been raided, everyone present would have known to dump the contents of whatever was in their glass into the tubs of water, ensuring a complete dilution of illegal liquor immediately."

My pride over The Bluff oozes from me, even after all these years.

I give June a raised eyebrow look. "Some places in town were nothing more than a wood floor and a jug of moonshine. Though we weren't known for a raucous good time, not like it was in some cities across the country, we had a thriving business at The Bluff. Given the building's proximity to the police station and city hall, loud music was out of the question. Instead, we played low, slow jazzy tunes that drew couples to their feet. I remember it like it was yesterday. I was dressed in a slinky, low-backed number that showed off my shapely figure."

I deliver an assured stare in June's direction. "I did have a fantastic figure at one time. You can trust me on that."

June's laugh sounds like a set of wind chimes, making me smile.

"I swear George's jaw dropped when I descended the stairs from my apartment."

A wide grin emerges, lifting my cheeks at the thought of that moment, the one where I knew I had done the right thing in acquiescing to George's insistence that I open The Bluff.

"George gave me a diamond bracelet that night." My shoulder lifts in a half-hearted shrug, though I keep my past desire for it to have been a ring tucked well out of sight from the girl. She doesn't need to know everything. "The bracelet was beautiful, and it was a sure sign that business was booming and he was proud of me for taking the plunge with The Bluff."

June sips from her water glass as she waits for me to continue. I suspect she is holding her tongue to ensure I don't hold mine, but I say nothing about it and continue on with my reverie, unable to stop.

"I was at home in my new operation. Between George, and the boys, and The Bluff, I thought I had found myself again. My life changed dramatically in 1922. I went from being a respectable, though likely pitied, spinster living on my parents' vineyard to becoming a bootlegger and speakeasy owner wearing fancy dresses, silk stockings, and fur-trimmed coats. I went from tasting wine to determine its readiness to securing illegal booze for profit."

I shake my head at the contradictory lifestyles. "It turned out that the apartment upstairs allowed me to move to and from The Bluff without ever having to walk out doors, and I soon found myself comfortable in a home all my own."

I pause, wondering if I've said too much.

"Nobody ever suspected?" June's question catches me off guard.

"No. It seems not. I filed the proper papers with the city, claiming the building was to be used for the small batch manufacture of perfume, and hung a sign to match above the door. I imagine that kept most suspicion off the place. Those beautiful bottles I mentioned. The ones behind the bar. They were varying shapes and sizes of perfume bottles, all of them filled with alcohol."

"That was clever of you."

A low chuckle alights from my chest. "I had even taken to opening scents and sprinkling them along the front and rear access points of the building twice a day for months in an effort to establish the location as a women's perfume factory. Channel No. 5, they were not, but the perfume emitted from within clearly did the trick in dissuading the curious from looking too closely at my operation. My resolve, or perhaps it was my fear, to remain undetected by dry agents pushed me as far as to make the occasional scented concoction myself. I actually shipped a crate or two a week to random addresses from the local post office. Since my fictional business was to sell to other businesses, I never had to contend with individual customers from town."

"You certainly thought of everything." Though she doesn't say so directly, I sense June's wheels are turning, wondering how, with such careful planning on my part, I landed myself in jail in the first place.

I wave off her comment. "By the end of The Bluff's opening night, George was the happiest I'd ever seen him. He was delighted by the night's success and seeing him so pleased made me the happiest I'd ever been too."

I pull myself from the sights and sounds of The Bluff and inhale the cool night air. "Well, when it comes to the 1920s, the high life was relative to whether you were embracing Prohibition or trying to outsmart it." She may not see me in the shadowy light, but I wink anyway. "I, of course, was trying to outsmart it."

June swivels the rocker to face the table and leans her elbows on the table's top.

"So besides The Bluff, there were the bootleg runs, of course. Traveling wherever I had to go to get the goods. Most times that was California, but I also made trips to Montana. Don't kid yourself June, being a bootlegger is a lot of work." Another laugh escapes at the thought of our well-timed vacation. "We traveled as far as New Orleans once for a stock load of Caribbean rum. That was the one and only time I actually felt like I was living the high life."

"You did? I didn't know it was safe to travel so far." June's eyes are wide in disbelief.

"Not our usual run, for sure, but once in a while we got the good stuff. George and I secretly called it a holiday, though the false wood-stacked truck puttering along at twenty miles per hour wouldn't have been my preference for a real adventure. But you do what you've got to do."

My body eases a little more into the cool of the evening, thankful for the reprieve from the oppressive heat but comforted by my sweater wrapped around me. "Took us nine days to get there and twelve to get back once we were loaded down and all."

"Was it worth the trip?" June sits back in the rocker, contemplating this new information. "I mean, how much can you make on one truckload of rum?"

"It was a different time. You have no idea how eager those who were ordered by law to go without their beloved drink of choice were desperate for a taste."

I can't hide my smile. "We were treated like celebrities when we arrived home."

June grins back at me as I continue. "That's when my nickname, the Bootleg Queen, really began to circulate among a select crowd of admirers who frequented my speakeasy, though I haven't the slightest idea when or how reporters got wind of it."

A bony finger points toward June, asserting my involvement in the success of the venture. "My being in the truck with George is what made the shipment a success. There wasn't a police officer going who would risk a scandal of having searched a vehicle with a female passenger, back in the day."

The chuckle rises from my chest, deep and low. "Only once, headed home with the false wood-stacked box loaded with fine Caribbean rum, were we stopped for a broken tail-light. George covered his hand with mine, hiding the lack of a wedding band, before lifting it for the police officer to see. He beamed a silly grin and announced we were on our honeymoon."

With a lull in the conversation before us, I feel June's readiness to launch into more questions. My heart beats faster in my chest. Have I said too much? I need time to consider what I've said and determine where to go from here.

Before she can say a thing, I cut her off. "It's getting late. Why don't you come back tomorrow with your notes typed up and I'll go over them then?"

June all but stumbles the words out. "Typed notes?"

"Yes, I assume you'll want a solid account of the things we've gone over today. And I'll need to see what you've taken from our conversation so I can approve them. Don't think I'll let any nonsense get past me."

Both of June's feet land on the porch floorboards with a thud, her back stiffening to defend her position. "That's not how this usually works. I gather all the information and then I write the article."

"Not this time. I want to see every note so I can make sure you've got it right. I do not intend to be misrepresented again."

The girl slumps, weariness oozing out of her. Popping the lid back on the cookies, June stands. "Well then, I better be going, since I've got unexpected homework to contend with."

I can tell she is miffed, so I tuck the chuckle that is threatening to emerge behind a solemn nod.

Having retrieved her bag from inside the house, June re-emerges on the porch with some cautioning words of her own. "I'll be back in the morning and we can start fresh then. But, Meg, I don't have oodles of time to spend out here if you aren't going to open up. You'll have to trust me enough to tell me what happened the day of the raid or I'll be gone by noon."

My only response is a single nod of my head. The girl can't comprehend. It's not her I don't trust. It's me.

The station wagon's headlights disappear, bumping over the potholes that line the now desolate road. The dust, stirred up by June's woodie, hits my nose, sending me back in time to a memory I had long tried to forget about.

A soft rustle glides past my legs, breaking me free of my thoughts. The cat has found its way back and is now ready to return to the comfort and safety of our little home. I stand, my knees threatening to give way, and shuffle toward the screen door, hopeful that sleep will have no trouble finding me tonight.

Twenty-Two

JULY 1923
ELKO, NEVADA

MEG

INCHING ALONG THE LOW CORRIDOR, MY NOSE itches with the aroma of decades-old, caked dirt. I use an outstretched hand as my guide. Not wishing to bloody myself on jagged rock, I follow close behind George as we make our first trip underground from The Bluff to the warehouse.

The tunnels are new for us. Despite having been dug, and then used by the original Chinese inhabitants, I resisted the hidden path well below the city's streets until we could no longer avoid taking advantage of it. George and the others voted the underground tunnels were the best option for supplying my speakeasy with booze, despite my objections.

Of course they did. I mumble my discontent, narrowly missing a boulder protruding from the makeshift walls. In an effort to keep my wits about me, I pinch my arm hard enough to curse, determined to rally my senses with camouflaged danger lurking at every turn within the shadows. It's hard to argue with their logic, given three other speakeasies in Elko have been raided and shut down in recent weeks. All of them garnering boisterous newspaper reports with beaming officials and barrels empty of their contents. All of the businesses shut down and boarded up for at least a year. That is something George was able to convince me was not an option. If The Bluff is forced to close, another opportunity for George and the rest of us ends with it.

The boys, seeing an opportunity to secure their livelihoods, and forever seeking to increase their share of profits and their turnover of bootlegged liquor, needed to find another way to avoid suspicion and keep everyone in business. Since I own the speakeasy, the tunnels offer a safer path forward, ensuring our mutual partnership remains prosperous. My displeasure at having to be here is made worse knowing that the boys aren't the ones having to trek around beneath the town, burrowing like a night crawler.

"Watch your head, here." George calls back over his shoulder with a hand placed high on a tight corner.

I follow his lead, keeping my disgruntled comments to myself. He was the only one to offer to go with me, after all. For that, I am grateful.

I feel a trickle of sweat as it snakes down my back toward my waistband. I cannot believe anyone would be inclined to use the tunnels at all, much less on a regular basis. The man who told us about their existence, while also providing the map George has clutched in his fist, is a descendant of those who frequented the tunnels. They were originally dug out and used as a way of traveling to visit friends and family during a time when it was against the law for Chinese residents to be seen in town after sunset.

The law itself, much like the one banning the consumption of alcohol, makes little sense to me. What a way for us to treat the workers who arrived in the country, ready to break their backs and build us a railway. I am thankful George saw fit to pay the man well for his knowledge and the map. But, when asked to go with us, the man took George's money and flatly refused, leaving me with an unsettled feeling.

"We're almost there." George, with his usual jovial demeanor, calls back in my direction.

My only reply is a grunt as I wipe moisture from my forehead with the back of my grimy hand.

It's easy to be cheery when you are raking in hundreds of thousands of dollars each year. George's businesses have always done well, even before Prohibition when he operated legitimate enterprises.

With the boom in bootlegging, though, his overall wealth has accumulated much more quickly than any of his other ventures have. Despite being a couple, George insists we keep our individual lodgings, finances, and lives separate when it comes to the outside world. To anyone outside of our little gang of misfits, we are two people who have nothing to do with one another.

I shouldn't be sour. He is generous when he sees fit to be, and his affection for me appears real. But I suspect George is far more successful than I am at actually having a life outside of us.

I push down my feelings on the topic, knowing from experience that trying to have a conversation about changing our current situation, to one of a more legal and binding status, is a guaranteed way to ensure George has urgent business out of town. Business that is sure to last for weeks on end. Long enough for me to have moved on from any conversation concerning the topic of marriage.

I can't say for certain, but I've surmised this venture through the tunnels, with the intended outcome being an increase in income for me via the speakeasy, is George's way of making things right between us. Little does he know that his money interests me far less than the thought of having him by my side for the rest of my life. A small sigh slips through my closed lips. Our differences on the subject seem more visible here in the darkened underground caves than they are in the light of day.

George's insistence that the tunnels would provide me with a proper income is his way of ensuring I will be financially taken care of. He worries over such things for me, and if I were to get to the heart of it, that is how he shows his love for me. If only he would realize it's him I want more than anything else in the world.

As soon as the supply issue and delivery to the speakeasy challenges are solved, he said, I'd be in fine shape to run a proper business. I expect he didn't notice that I had been running a proper business, apparently, just not one of grand enough scale for his liking. For the past several months, I've kept my head down and been happy to operate a moderate establishment with trusted clientele. But, when George learned of another speakeasy owner earning profits from buying a gallon of bootlegged whiskey for one dollar, then turning around and selling it for fifty cents a shot, the dollar signs must have danced in his dreams. There was nothing I could say to deter his enthusiasm on the plan growing inside his head.

A whoosh of cool air lingers past me as George opens the door with a hard shove of his shoulder. Following the steps built into the wall, we climb the few feet up and raise the trap door. We are exactly where the map said we'd be: inside George's warehouse filled with crates of contraband ready to be moved.

Twenty-Three

AUGUST 1955
ELKO, NEVADA

JUNE

THE NEXT MORNING, I WAKE WITH THE SUN. NOT because I want to, but rather because the motel room curtains leave much to be desired when it comes to blocking out the early morning rays. I was up past midnight, writing my notes out by hand. Though the portable typewriter I borrowed from the newspaper office is stashed in the car's rear storage compartment, I couldn't bring myself to punch away on the thing and risk disturbing other guests in adjacent rooms.

I glance over my notes with bleary eyes before enjoying a leisurely shower and pulling on a pair of black pedal pushers and a patterned sleeveless button-up with a tie at the waist. Having spent yesterday afternoon in a freshly pressed dress, I opt for something with comfort instead of fashion in mind, certain Meg won't care in the slightest either way.

After yesterday's stilted beginning, I'm eager to get the answers to my questions. I am certain Meg knows more than she's letting on about who was responsible for her going to jail, but deciphering what she knows is something I have yet to succeed at. The thing that troubles me most, and was cause for my less than restful sleep, is the suspicion that Meg is protecting someone who doesn't deserve her silence.

She said it herself. George told her to protect the tribe first. My desire to support Meg in re-establishing the facts of the situation is of little use if Meg herself has no interest in doing so. If that's what I'm faced with again this morning, I am afraid my goal of writing a feature article that redeems Meg's character, and corrects the inaccuracy of the historical record, is over, and with it my front-page article.

An hour later, I step out of my motel room door and slide my sunglasses in place. I relish the fresh feeling the new day provides, regardless of the fact that the summer heat is likely to do me in and hold me hostage within the next few hours.

Thankful Benny's Coffee Shop is attached to the motel, I tuck the car keys into my bag and make a beeline for the coffee shop. Given Meg's lackluster, and somewhat suspect offering of food yesterday, I decide to purchase two full breakfasts with coffee, hoping the gesture will go far in smoothing over any bumpy patches with the woman this morning.

With the order placed, I sit on a barstool at the counter and sip a steaming cup of coffee. Paging through my notes, I try to examine my questions through Meg's perspective. With the awareness of someone else's involvement in her actions thrumming through my mind, I see my questions as potentially threatening to Meg. She might even view them as hostile if she's protecting someone she loves. Though I sense her sharp tongue exists for the benefit of self-preservation, I have no interest in being on the receiving end of another lashing. I'll have to tread more carefully today.

With breakfast lain with care on the car's floorboards, I drive ten minutes out of town toward Meg's house, my mind going over what I know, while all the things I still have questions about poke at me from every direction. Coffee permeates the car's interior as I snag a page from my bag and center it over the steering wheel between both hands while I navigate the sleepy streets of Elko's suburbs. The page is my wish list of questions. The inquiries I hope with all my might Meg will be inclined to speak with me about this morning.

My plentiful questions far outweigh the current knowledge I've gathered about Meg's life, but there is something she has yet to confirm that is doing a fine job of making me feel uneasy. My bottom lip settles between my teeth, a sure sign that my confidence in acquiring this story is slipping through my fingers. Disliking the sensation of feeling out of control, I give my head a firm shake and straighten my shoulders. All I can do is try again. Maybe after a solid night of sleep, Meg will be in the right frame of mind to share her entire story with me, details and all.

Meg is sitting on the front porch, the same place I left her as I drove away last night. A pang of guilt clutches my chest as I park the car in the driveway. Surely, she didn't stay out on the porch all night. I take a deep breath and steady myself before opening the car door.

"Good morning," I call across the large square of dirt that I am certain, at one time, grew grass. Adding a teasing tone, I try my hand at nonchalance. "You didn't stay out here all night, did you?"

Meg shields her eyes with one hand. Relief washes over

me when I'm greeted with the small lift of her lips and a subtle shake of her head.

I retrieve our breakfast, placing the bag and two coffees on the car's hood while tucking the loose page of notes back in with the others in my bag. There'll be time enough for those, I tell myself while pasting on a cheerful expression and turning toward Meg with breakfast in hand.

"I thought you might like some food." I raise the brown bag in my hand. "And coffee," I add, hoping I've assumed correctly. Climbing the steps to the porch, I continue. "I wasn't sure if you drank coffee, but I know I could use some this morning."

"Thank you." Meg gestures for me to place it on the wobbly table. "That is kind of you."

Fresh start. Check.

I place the food down. My desire to make this work between us rises up and snatches the victory of having received polite, and dare I think, possibly kind words directed toward me and my offering.

I lift the containers out of the bag. The scent of fried potatoes, fresh buttered toast, bacon, and scrambled eggs waft up to greet me. I arrange a plastic fork and knife for each of us, both sets wrapped in a tidy little bundle complete with a paper napkin, on the table in front of both chairs before peeling back the individual paper coffee cup handles and securing them together as one.

Meg watches the steam rise from the cups before standing abruptly and moving toward the house. "I'll get us some cutlery."

"Oh, they've given us these. They are kind of nifty." I lift the small pieces of plastic to eye level before returning it to the table.

"Nifty doesn't necessarily mean proper. I may be a vine-yard girl, but I wasn't raised in a barn." Meg scowls over her shoulder before slipping past the screen door and into the house.

I'm taking a sip of coffee when she reappears.

"I prefer the real thing." Meg settles herself at the table and lifts two forks in the air with a sheepish expression that tells me she is apologizing for her sharp tongue, despite disagreeing with my choice of utensil.

I smile at the exchange, remembering my mother's much similar response to the introduction of plastic cutlery. She had had little to say when I teased her by asking if we should start bringing our own forks and knives from home on any given day, in case we stopped for food along the way.

Hunger overcomes me and I dive into the meal, eager to satisfy the grumbling in my stomach. Several mouthfuls later, I notice Meg is only picking at her food. I am about to ask her if everything is alright when I hear a meow coming from somewhere near my feet.

I duck my head and spot the black cat sitting under the table. "What's your cat's name?" I ask, determined to make light breakfast conversation.

"He doesn't have a name." Meg bends at the waist, scooping her eggs out of the container and onto the porch for the cat to enjoy. "He showed up one day and insisted on being let in." She rubs the top of his head before adding, "and then he insisted on being fed, the cheeky rascal."

"So, you adopted him. How sweet." I take another bite. "He must be new then, if he doesn't have a name."

"No. Not new. Just no name." Meg shrugs. "I call him Kitty if I need to call him anything at all. We mostly stay out of one another's way, though he knows to come in before it gets too late and he has a knack for being present when food is being offered."

I smile at the interesting pairing, and consider whether it's a lack of affection or a determined sense of individual responsibility that has led to this strange companionship with the cat. Meg returns her attention to moving her food around with her fork, seldom taking a bite.

"I have those notes you asked for." I take another sip of coffee, grateful for the infusion of caffeine. "My typewriter would have been too noisy, so I didn't type them, but I've written them all down and I have a list of questions we can work through today. I thought if we established a direction, we'd be able to cover more ground with the time we have. Before you say anything, I want you to know I'm not trying to be impertinent, Meg. I only hope to make things as easy as possible, for both of us."

Pulling the notes from my bag, I hand them to Meg as I focus on finishing the last few bites of my breakfast.

Pushing aside her food container, with most of the breakfast still intact, Meg turns her attention to the pages before her. A few moments later, a faint smile graces her otherwise stern expression. A surge of relief floods through me and I exhale, grateful to have finally won the woman over. I wait for Meg to make the next move.

Now we can really get started.

"This is well thought out." Meg meets my gaze. "Okay then. What would you like to know first?"

Twenty-Four

MEG

I WATCH THE GIRL'S EXPRESSION AS IT TURNS FROM anxious to delighted. Bringing breakfast was a thoughtful gesture. Regardless of whether or not I can eat the food, I have to give her credit for the thought.

The cat, having finished my eggs, weaves his way through my legs, purring his satisfaction at having been offered the treat. I caught the perplexed look on June's face when I spoke of the cat. But the two of us, the cat and I, are well-suited to one another, both of us comfortable with small doses of interaction. The girl may not comprehend such a thing, but when you've lived alone for decades, it becomes more difficult to let others into the world of solitude you've created for yourself.

June clears her throat, interrupting my thoughts. "If it's alright with you, I'd like to learn more about George. I've got an idea of who he was to you, but if you can fill me in on the details of the raid, and whether he was involved or not, that would help me understand things from your perspective more clearly. Then, if it's alright with you, we can move on from there."

I shift in my seat, preparing for what is to come. "If you must." It took me several hours of brooding, but somewhere in the middle of a sleepless night, I committed to the idea of speaking freely about George. Truly, there is little more to say. Most of what the girl would want to know about the man can be found in the newspaper archives she's so fond of riffling through.

Tossing and turning did little to show me another way around the topic. Last night, we shared a few lighthearted moments as I spoke about The Bluff and George's involvement in my life. By the time she had driven off, I was certain June would bring him up again. This time, instead of dodging her interest in George, I've decided I am ready. I know precisely what I will say.

I steel myself and take a sip of coffee. The strong, warm roast tickles my nose, and I am reminded how much I've missed the beverage. Savoring the aroma, a gurgle in my stomach tells me to take it slow. Both the coffee, and the topic of George, need to be doled out in small amounts for either of them to have a shot at being digested comfortably.

"I met George the first day I set foot in Elko." The smile and the memory come easily for me since, in that moment, he was my knight in shining armor. "He was the most dashing man I had ever laid eyes on. Suave, confident, with bright green eyes that made you feel extra special when he shone them in your direction."

I look to June to explain further. "It's not entirely common for a man of Italian heritage to have green eyes, you see. That was partly what drew me to him. Well, that and the way he made me feel."

June relaxes into the rocking chair, rousing it into motion as she sips her coffee.

"My brother, Matteo, introduced us. Well—actually, come to think of it, George introduced himself. He was seldom shy. He oozed confidence like a grapevine drips tears in springtime." A soft chuckle is cut short by a squeeze centered over my chest.

I place a hand where I imagine my weary lungs lie and massage gently while continuing. "You see, I had telephoned Matteo from a roadside stop once I was en route to Elko. I arrived at the Elko bus depot with all that I owned having been shoved into two duffle bags by my father. So, there I was, exhausted from the bus trip from Napa, looking utterly pathetic with my ramshackle of belongings and a tear-stained face."

My gaze searches the distance beyond the dusty front yard, tugging the memory to the forefront of my mind.

"Matteo greeted me as I stepped off the bus and as we made our way toward the parking lot, he explained he couldn't bring me home with him, not yet. Not to worry, he said, he had made other arrangements. Someone he was acquainted with in the side business, as he liked to call his black market activities, would help me out. He assured me the man was a decent sort and a stand-up guy, given his dealings with him."

I sneak a glance in June's direction, gauging her response.

"I gave my brother a sharp look, immediately offended that he would pass me off to some man he barely knew. Matteo put an arm around my shoulders, telling me he trusted the man. 'I haven't known him long,' he said, 'but he's polite and well-mannered, and Italian, to boot. You'll like him.'"

Out of the corner of my periphery, I watch as June's mouth turns toward a frown.

"Before I could object further, we were standing in front of George, him with his hand extended in my direction. 'I'm George Fumagalli. Welcome to Elko. Your brother here tells me you are looking for a place to stay and maybe even a job. I'm happy to say, I can help you with both.'"

"What did you say?" June's question is subdued, but pleading. "Please tell me your brother didn't simply hand you off to a complete stranger."

"He did. Matteo told me I was in good hands and he was a phone call away if I needed anything."

"He didn't?" June's mouth drops open as the coffee she's holding stalls in its trajectory toward her lips.

"He really did." I wave off the girl's worry like I'm swatting at a fly.

I sense June has a keener grasp on Matteo than I might have given her credit for. Somehow, she has read between the lines and is drawing her own conclusions and doubts about the relationship with my brother.

"In all honesty, with George's face lit up in a smile so warm, it was easy to gravitate toward him. He made me feel safe and so I went with him. He took me under his wing immediately and whisked me away to a new life. He set me up in the local hotel until I got my footing. He even gave me a job—within his bootleg operation."

I let the thoughts percolate through my mind. "I never did set foot in Matteo's house, though. Wasn't invited for Thanksgiving or Christmas. Never had the chance to develop a relationship with his wife or fully grown children, despite living in the same town for many years." I steal a glance in the girl's direction, monitoring her reaction to this admission.

My heart takes a tiny leap of relief at seeing June's mouth fall open. Though I am not quite ready to confide in her with all of it, I am pleased to see her troubled by the blatant banishment from my family.

Understanding the reality of my brother's life, I try to explain Matteo's logic. "It wasn't entirely as cold-hearted as it may seem. When you're someone who is skirting the law with black market activities, you have to be prepared to distance yourself from family, if only to protect your loved ones from prosecution, if things were to spiral out of control. I had already lost my parents' affections, and it didn't take long for me to understand the consequences of my actions. I was, in the end, at fault."

"But didn't your brother's family know of his involvement in shipping sacramental wine to Nevada for sale on the black market?" June's forehead creases in question.

I shake my head. "Matteo was a master at keeping secrets, even from me."

We sip our coffee in silence as the emotional dust settles over the words I've spoken.

"Anyway, once I was working with George, I was busy enough to push thoughts of what I was missing out on, in terms of family, aside. After my parents passed away, I could return to California without the worry of being discovered, and proceeded to run all sorts of bootlegged alcohol from California to Nevada. George traveled with me in the beginning as he introduced me around to his customers, but as soon as I proved my abilities, I was given my marching orders and off I went."

"So, you were bootlegging before opening the speakeasy?" June places her cup on the wobbly table.

"Technically, I began bootlegging wine from Napa for my brother while living on the vineyard. It was the summer of 1922 when we entered the sacramental wine black market. The speakeasy was opened at George's urgings in December 1922. By then..." My eyes flick up to find June watching me intently.

"By then, as you know, George and I were romantically involved." I thought after all these years, I'd be too weathered to feel the intensity of a remembered stolen moment, but here I sit, imagining my cheeks are flaming as my mind dances through an imaginary highlight reel of scenes between George and me.

I think back to the day George's attention on me turned romantic. I was already smitten since his confident, can-do attitude put me at ease while making me feel cared for from the moment I first met him. It didn't hurt that the man was ruggedly handsome in a mischievous way that made me want to see what he was capable of. He laughed easily and often, helping me rediscover my muted sense of humor. It was our shared enjoyment of quick thinking that cemented our attraction to one another, our banter drawing lingering smiles from both of us.

He came to see me at the hotel he was paying for, stepping into my room with a warm smile and a list of instructions for my first bootleg run. I imagine the worry over my first run was emanating from me like a heat wave while making me feel reckless, as if I were living on the edge. George stepped forward to offer me a reassuring squeeze of my arm. I mistook his intention and leaned in. His eyes searched mine with an intensity I had never felt before.

A corner of my mouth lifts up at the memory. In all the years that we knew one another, it was the only time I saw George flustered. He didn't step away or apologize, he simply asked if I was sure. He babbled on about impropriety and not wanting to put me in an uncomfortable situation. Cautioning me on the potential danger of working together while sharing other things. The more he stammered, the more interested I became in him. Within moments, his lips were on mine and we were falling onto my single sized bed as if the world was ending and these were our last moments of life itself.

The growing warmth in my cheeks pulls me back to the porch and June's presence. I place a palm against the flush and sneak a glance in the girl's direction.

June's head bobs up and down. "I see. So, you continued that way until the raid in January 1926?"

"That is correct." My voice is full of gravel, though I choose to blame it on the lengthy conversation instead of the raw emotions swirling around me.

"Did George have anything to do with the raid?" With the lay of the land behind us, June lunges toward the heart of her questions.

There is no turning back now. I promised myself I would tell her the truth. If I am not honest with the girl, she won't understand who I am. "Yes, George was involved with all aspects of the operation, since it was his warehouse and all."

"But he didn't go to jail. He was arrested but pled not guilty and didn't go to jail." June leans forward in the rocker, her fingers drumming anxiously on her thighs.

"If you've scoured the newspapers from the day as you've said you have, then surely you read about George's history of evading prosecution?" The girl looks at me with a furrowed brow. "Maybe it sounds absurd, but honestly, we used to laugh about it, really. George had a knack for getting what he wanted. At any given time, there were charges against him, but none of them ever stuck."

I try to give the girl context of how life was in 1926. "You have to remember, he was also involved in legitimate businesses around Elko and his Prohibition activities were played down by authorities. It was assumed he was a small time player, out for a bit of fun. In later years, as the dry agents cracked down across the state, George was held up more frequently, but even then, he was out on bail so often that his arrests became a stream of revenue for the city."

"I don't understand." June leans in further, and I wonder if she is at risk of falling out of the rocking chair.

"George never went to jail for any of it. I'm not sure his polished oxfords ever graced the cement floor of a single jail cell. I certainly didn't expect him to go to jail for the raid either. He was too smart for that."

A hand washes over my face as I gather my thoughts and try again to explain how things were done during Prohibition, so June will understand. "Besides posting his own bail, George either paid off prosecutors, witnesses, or judges. Bribery was simply part of the business. Sometimes he paid for trips out of town for those set to testify against him, ensuring they wouldn't be available when the case went to court. He was a master at playing people against one another, doing whatever he had to do to get what he needed."

As the words fall from my lips, I can no longer hide from

the truth I've been determined to hold at bay. I've been afraid to dig too deeply into this line of thinking all these years, worried if I put voice to my thoughts, I'd be breaking my heart all over again. Clear as day, the truth stares back at me now. George saved himself in 1926, just like he always did.

I shake the realization from my awareness, determined not to give myself away to the girl. I switch gears and offer a nugget I hope she'll find entertaining. "He was even known for destroying contraband right in front of Prohibition agents. One time, he simply asked to see a bottle he'd been found with. He took one glance at it before smashing it against a pipe and destroying the evidence. All the officers could do was hang their heads and bemoan their gullibility at being outsmarted."

I expect June to laugh, or at least crack a smile, but she remains frozen in place, her mind probably whirring with the stories I've recounted. I shift in my chair, cognizant of the girl's quick mind while awareness creeps in.

It is too late to stop what I've started now.

Twenty-Five

JUNE

The sun is creeping toward the porch, the shadows on the wood slats being washed away by the brightness of the day. I am contemplating where to take my questions next. George, according to Meg, is an interesting and somewhat elusive character. What concerns me most is how intricately her life was once entwined with his. Though she doesn't say as much, I suspect theirs was more of a one-sided love affair, and if my suspicions are correct, it was also a relationship that may have landed Meg in jail for his wrongdoings.

"Did you ever speak to George again? Do you know where he is now?" My questions tumble out over top of one another. The reporter in me would love nothing more than to track the man down and extract answers from him.

"I never spoke to him again." Meg shakes her head as her lips purse in what I suspect is disappointment. Or could it be distaste? Meg peers for a few minutes over the porch rail into the distance before speaking again. "He married a girl half my age before I was released from jail."

"He what?" I am ready to bolt straight up from my chair. This I did not see coming. "The scoundrel." The words fly from my lips, lined with incredulity, and perhaps a little venom.

Meg offers me a tight smile. "That's one word for him. I'd be lying if I said I hadn't come up with a few others of my own over the years."

"Where is he now?" I feel my fingernails as they dig into the wood arm rests of the rocking chair.

"You can find him in the Elko City Cemetery." Meg lifts a shoulder in a *what can I say* gesture. "Died about twenty years ago, now."

I slump back in my seat, irritation toward a man I've never laid eyes on forcing me backward.

"Well, that about does it for the story of George and me." Meg stands. Gathering the breakfast containers and coffee cups from the table, she moves toward the screen door. "I'll put the kettle on. We can have tea."

I'd love to know more. How did he die? Was he ever punished for his illegal activities? What happened to his bootleg enterprise? There is so much more when it comes to George, but if I've learned anything in the last twenty-four hours, it's that pressing Meg after she's said she's done is an ill-advised course of action. Instead, I hope to get to the heart of why she was the only one to go to jail back in 1926. I grab my bag and hand-written notes, and follow her into the house.

The morning's slight breeze has cooled the living room to a reasonable temperature after yesterday's heat, and I'm thankful for the reprieve. Meg moves toward the kitchen, the cat following close on her heels in what I assume is an attempt to gain more to eat.

I take my seat, same as before, upon the lumpy sofa and wait for Meg to return. My mind spins with the contradicting descriptions of George. From what she first told me, I would have guessed him to be a like-able man, but with what I know now, all I can surmise is he hid his intentions well. He may have enjoyed Meg's company, and all the perks that likely went with it, but I can't imagine he cared for her like he should have, not given the way he abandoned her in the end.

My body hums with frustration. The question I want to ask is on the tip of my tongue as Meg putters around in the kitchen. I hear the kitchen tap fill the kettle, and the cups bumping against one another, as she retrieves them from the cupboard.

Agitation moves through me, showing itself with the repetitive thrumming of my heel against the hardwood floor. I can't ask Meg anything if she remains in the kitchen, but if I'm being honest, that isn't my greatest concern. Instead, it's the fact that I'm squirming with the indelicate question pressing in on me. How do I tactfully ask Meg if she believes George sacrificed her freedom to save his own skin?

It appears she loved the man, warts and all, though I suspect his outward appearance and charm were far less bullfrog and much more Clark Gable, and I'm almost certain he used those attributes to his advantage. I shake my head at the internal argument. Regardless of how Meg felt about the man, I must ask her if she blames him. Impertinent or not, I simply don't see another way around it if I'm going to understand the full extent of the story.

I stand to help as Meg enters the room. A wood tray

loaded with a teapot, mismatched china cups, sugar, and cream rests in her hands. I spot a familiar pattern on the teapot and one of the teacups. "Oh, how nice." I point to the tray. "My Grandma Ruth had some of the same china pattern as that one there."

Meg bends at the waist, lowering the tray to the coffee table.

"I say some, because the set was never complete. It had five teacups instead of six, and I never saw a matching teapot like yours, though." I dismiss the oddity of the missing pieces of china from my grandmother's cabinet as my mind ruminates on what I feel compelled to ask Meg next.

"My Grandma Ruth told me the incomplete set came from her mother-in-law after she passed, so yours must be quite an antique as well. It's funny really. She claimed she'd only met her mother-in-law once and I've never understood how such a thing was possible. To not know your family, do you know what I mean?"

I shake my head at the thought of my family conundrum at the same time Meg's gaze veers from the tray to me. Her hands tremble, eliciting a clanging of all the things on the tray as she races to set what must be a heavy tray down.

"We never figured out where the missing pieces went. It's a beautiful pattern—"

My words falter as one end of the tray dips lower in Meg's hands, and before either of us can stop it, the tray's corner hits with a hard thwack against the coffee table. Hot tea pours from the pot, spilling over Meg's table, a stack of outdated *Life* magazines, and something that I assume is a scrapbook of sorts.

Meg releases the rest of the tray to the table while my hands dive into my bag, reaching for the tissues I always keep handy. "Not to worry. We'll get this cleaned up," I say as I jump into action and dab at the table and the scrapbook surmising the personal item will be far more important than an outdated issue of *Life*.

Moving to the kitchen and back, Meg brings a tea towel and kneels with some difficulty to help me mop up the wet. With the table wiped free of the worst puddles, I peel open the scrapbook to assess the damage. Careful not to tear the damp edges, and with the book resting precariously in my hands, several newspaper clippings slide from within onto the living room floor.

"I apologize, I was only—" My words are cut short as I recognize *The Carson City News* logo. My eyes roam over the scattered clippings. It takes a moment before I'm aware. Each one is an article I have written. "What are these?" My attention darts between the scrapbook and Meg, my mind whirring to catch up with what is before me.

Meg, looking up from her bent position at the coffee table, is unable to hide her surprise. "I—I was doing my research on you before agreeing to the interview. Thought it was prudent to know more about the girl who'd sought me out."

Believable enough.

I gather the clippings up. When my gaze lands on my most recent article, the one awarded a prime location on the front-page of the newspaper, I feel the air leave my body. My biggest achievement in my career to date, but also the one missing my name from the byline. I was over the moon about my story and unable to contain my excitement at showing my parents how their daughter had written something worthy of the front page. I was convinced my father would be proud of me and finally see how serious I am about my career. But, when the paper arrived on the doorstep with my article front and center, the pride I was filled with deflated like a popped balloon as I saw my name had been stripped from its proper place and instead replaced by "Carson City News Reporter."

Oh, the words I had for my editor that morning. He gave me some lame song and dance, indicating a delicate story such as the one I provided wouldn't be well received by the reading public should the author be a woman. I fumed my way toward the archives room, intent on finding a story that wouldn't be stolen out from under me.

With the sting of my accomplishment being stolen from me still rushing through my veins, a new awareness dawns on me. I hold up my front-page article for Meg to see. "And this one? This doesn't even have my name on it. How did you know it was mine?"

The woman has the decency to look befuddled.

"Why do you have these, Meg? Is there something you aren't telling me?" I hear my voice rising like an ocean wave about to crest. I square my jaw and tuck my chin, trying to maintain my composure. "It must have taken some effort, not to mention expense, to obtain *The Carson City News* in Elko. You were looking into me before I arrived in Elko. Why?"

"I—I only figured it was yours, given the similar writing style." She is flustered. Caught in her lies. And we both know it.

I can feel the progress we've made slipping through my fingers. "How are we supposed to trust one another if you won't tell me what's really going on?" I place the scrapbook on the coffee table with a thud. "Why do you have every article I've ever written? Surely, a simple phone call to the newspaper would have told you I was a legitimate reporter working for them." I resist the urge to cross my arms over my chest and tap my toe against the hardwood floor as my frustration builds.

Meg kneels there, in front of the coffee table, her eyes downcast and her shoulders hunched. "I wanted to know who you are, is all." A moment of silence passes between us before she steals a cautious glimpse in my direction. "That's the truth, June."

The familiar sensation of being manipulated slinks up my spine, wrenching my thoughts back to the argument I had with my father. I run a hand through my hair in an effort to settle the thrumming of what I'm sure is going to be a whopper of a headache. A strangled laugh rumbles from my lips. The irony isn't lost on me.

"I don't understand why everyone in my life seems to want to manage me. If it isn't you keeping me in the dark and avoiding my questions at every turn, it's my editor, pulling my name off my work to appease a social constraint that, quite frankly, should no longer exist."

I shake my head, disagreeing ahead of the words spilling forth, the frustration with my father that's been building over the months choosing this moment to bubble up within me. "When I'm at home, my father continually implies that he knows best, guiding me in a direction that screams, I should give up on my dream of becoming a reporter like Nellie Bly. He would much rather see me marry than succeed in any career. Don't you see? I want to be taken seriously, as a reporter and as a woman. I don't want my life to be dictated by others. Didn't we earn these rights when we won the right to vote? Or are women only permitted a voice in the capacity of an electoral ballot and not truly in our daily lives? You, of all people, Meg, should know how it feels to be silenced and coerced into submission. I can't stand for it."

I don't even try to restrain the huff as it sails from my lips. Childish, perhaps, but still warranted. "All I want is for us to be honest with one another."

Meg places both palms flat against the coffee table, an indication that my words have touched a nerve. "I'm sure you do."

Twenty-Six

MEG

Heaving myself to standing, using the coffee table to help leverage me from my knees, takes more effort than I'd like. The girl is furious, and I contemplate whether any words I say will help. She isn't far off with her accusations. This I must admit. I knew who she was before she stepped foot in Elko yesterday afternoon, but the truth is I do want to know who she is. I had even mused that perhaps she could be the one to chronicle my life. I am no great historical figure, that's for certain, but a quiet memoir might help convince me, once and for all, that my life was not in vain.

She isn't wrong about my being silenced and coerced either, though I fear I am equally to blame in that regard. I wish I could have been stronger, had more gumption, like June does. In the end, when it came to the girl, I convinced myself I was protecting her from the pain the truth might bring. But I see it now. I was only protecting myself from the uncertainty of it all.

My chest squeezes, pushing out a sharp cough that takes my breath away. I splash a few drops of tea into a cup and gulp it down to quell the hacking cough I've come to anticipate in moments like these, while June continues to do angry laps around what sparse floor space my living room affords.

The tea does little to ease my discomfort, barely wetting my throat. I step back, bracing one hand against the wall. I cover my mouth with the other hand just in time for a flurry of deep rattling coughs to break free of my failing lungs. Why now? The question pesters me as I try to make sense of why my condition has decided to make itself known today, of all days.

June stops mid-stride and wheels an indignant expression in my direction. Her face morphs into concern as her gaze meets mine. "Are you alright? Can I get you anything? A glass of water?"

I hold up my hand. "I'm fine. Just a tickle." I push the words out before the cough takes over, proving me wrong again.

The coughing fit doubles me over at the waist as my worry over what I have yet to do fills every fiber of my being. I taste blood in my mouth and swipe at my lips with the soaked tea towel still clutched in my hand. I am too late. I fear I am running out of time for both June and the truth. Stubborn, that's what I've been. Too pigheaded for my own good.

June is beside me now, a gentle hand on my back as the cough turns from rattling to wheezing. Every breath feels heavier than the last. I curse the time I've wasted. Pussyfooting around the past is doing neither of us any good. She needs to know. The girl has to understand. She is the only one who can.

Forcing my body upright, I am gasping for air but desperate to tell the girl everything. Clutching June's arms, my lips form shapes, but nothing resembling words comes out. A heightened level of vexation blooms within me as I see my fate laid out before me. Time is running out.

"Meg, it's going to be okay." June is coaxing me toward the sofa. "Meg, can you hear me?"

June lowers me to the sofa, and I see her lips moving. I hear my name, but the rest is all echoes and whispers of garbled sound. How did I let it come to this? I should have been more courageous. That has always been my problem. All my life I've been brave at the wrong times and for the wrong reasons.

I feel the back of my head resting against the sofa's cushions, my soul knowing I've wasted any time I had left. My chance to tell June the truth is slipping through my fingers, and with it, all hope of clearing my name once and for all.

June's face is inches from my own, her warm hands cradling my head in what I assume is an effort to calm me. I can't understand a word she is saying. The look of anguish on her face when a dabbed tissue to my lips turns red with blood is like a knife to my heart. The poor girl never asked for this. I can't bear what I've done to her.

She moves from me to the side table faster than my brain can register and the last thing I see before closing my eyes to the spinning room is June, telephone in hand and lips moving.

～

I ASSUME TIME HAS PASSED, though I am not aware of how much. A man in a white shirt and black jacket is standing over me, two fingers holding my wrist as he examines a small watch. The coughing has subsided but has left in its place a fatigue heavy enough to keep me glued to the sofa, unable to lift a finger.

The man pats my shoulder while giving me a reassuring smile. He turns his attention to June, who is hovering nervously at the foot of the sofa, worry coating every inch of the girl. After a few shared words, they each take hold of either end of the coffee table and move it out of the way. All I can do is watch, not understanding, as they clear a path from the front door to the sofa.

When I finally realize what is happening, I dig my elbows into the sofa cushions and try with all my might to push myself to sitting. Determined not to be uprooted from my home, I struggle to prove I am well enough to remain in place.

June is at my side in an instant. "Meg, just rest now. They're bringing a portable bed in. They want to take you to the hospital. Do you understand?" The girl seems calmer now that help has arrived. I am certain I scared the life out of her with all that racket and the blood. Oh my, the blood, I am sure that terrified her, as it did me the first time I saw it. I must take control of the situation.

"I'm fine." The strength it takes to utter two words, neither of them above a croak of a whisper, catches me by surprise. I don't sound or feel fine, but with little time to waste, I must do all I can to ensure June doesn't leave Elko without knowing the truth.

A rumble of sound turns my head as a cot on wheels is rolled into my house. Bumping over the threshold before narrowly missing scraping the wall, the two men position the bed beside me and lower it to the same height as the sofa. I've never seen such a contraption, and my wariness of it must be evident as the man with the watch bends forward to explain what is about to happen.

"Mrs. Bruno, we're going to transfer you to this cot. Then we'll take you to the hospital. Okay?"

Here we go again, with the *Mrs.* I roll my eyes and let out an annoyed, though muffled, huff. Every woman over the age of twenty-five is assumed to be widowed, married, or about to be married. I can see June's point clearly now. Her frustration at being forced into a box of someone else's making is one more thing we have in common. Admiration for the girl blooms within me.

June steps forward. "Actually, it's Miss Bruno." June winks at me, a knowing grin curving her lips. "She is averse to the title of Mrs."

The second man is holding a clipboard and making what I assume are notes about me. Without missing a beat, June points to his clipboard. "Please be sure to mark that on her chart. I can assure you, Miss Bruno will be far more amenable to the hospital staff if they refer to her as such."

Despite the new-fangled cot being the same height as the sofa, the transfer over from one to the other is far more involved than my pride or my patience has tolerance for. Several minutes later, I am strapped in and rolling toward my front door.

"Wait." My voice sounds as though I've swallowed a handful of gravel. The cot stops moving all the same. "June."

June steps closer, and I lift my strapped-in wrist as high as it will go. She takes my hand in hers. "What is it, Meg?"

I feel the tears as they gather in my eyes. "Don't go."

The girl squeezes my hand reassuringly. "Everything is going to be alright. I'll come back and visit you once you've recovered. Okay?"

I shake my head. "Please. Don't go." The tears slide down, tracking an expedited path to the cot's white linen.

June's sharp inhale of breath confirms she suspected all was actually going to be okay. Oh, how I miss the innocence of youth.

"Stay. I will tell you everything." Quiet, but determined, I force the words out in a garbled whisper.

June's bottom lip slides between her teeth, her worry showing itself. A single nod of her head tells me she will do as I ask.

"Thank you." I offer a weak smile and an even weaker squeeze to her hand. "No more stalling."

A cough bursts through, but I push back with everything I've got. "You deserve to know the truth."

"Okay, Miss Bruno. We need to get you to the hospital." The man with the clipboard slides the cot forward before the two men lift me, cot and all, over the threshold and down the front porch steps into the bright sunlit day.

I can see June, holding the screen door open, contemplating the options before her. By the time I am being slid into the back of the ambulance, she spurs into action. "I'm coming too." With her bag gripped tight in one hand, June slams the front door closed behind her.

Twenty-Seven

JUNE

"Truth. What truth?" I whisper the words under my breath as I slide into the passenger seat of the ambulance. My hands are trembling. I try to still them by holding my bag on top of my lap. Whether it's Meg's rather unsettling coughing fit or the mention of my deserving to know the truth, I am not sure. All I'm confident of in this moment is my time with Meg is not over yet.

The man with the clipboard climbs in and starts the engine, shooting me a sympathetic smile as he puts the vehicle in drive. I glance over my shoulder through the small window into the back of the ambulance where Meg lies, her cot on wheels locked into place.

The ambulance driver takes it slow down the pot-hole riddled street, weaving around as many craters as he can while keeping his gaze fixed straight ahead. Grateful his concentration lies elsewhere, I am free to mull over the thoughts running amok inside my head. Two things, in particular, make little sense to me.

Meg has newspaper clippings of articles I've written going back as far as my first story almost a year ago. How can that be? I didn't even telephone her until a few weeks ago. Having never heard of the woman until I came across the archived articles on the 1926 raid in Elko, I had no reason to know who she was nor did she have reason, I assume, to know who I am. Something doesn't add up here.

Then, according to Meg, there must be some truth I deserve to know. I can't imagine anything other than these two pieces of information having something to do with one another. But what?

My rambling mind is interrupted by a quick rap on the window leading to the back of the ambulance. I turn in time to see the ambulance attendant motioning to the driver, his index finger pointed up and circling.

The driver flips a switch on the dashboard, spurring the vehicle into action. Lights flash and a siren wails. Adding to my unease, the driver presses down on the gas pedal, increasing our speed. I release my gripped fingers, turning in my seat to peer into the back of the ambulance.

Meg's torso is propped up. But with the rolling cot being elevated at a slight angle, the woman's expression is shielded from my view. All I can see is the attendant holding a mask over her mouth and nose while adjusting a valve on a large tank.

"What's happening? Is she okay?" My voice is frantic with an uncontrollable wobble to it.

"We'll be there soon." The driver glances in my direction. "Try not to worry. She's in capable hands."

The siren's scream echoes my distress while the fast pace

has me bumping all over the seat as I try to catch a glimpse of the woman behind me. "Come on, Meg." I say to no one in particular.

Spurred by the fear that I may never know Meg's truth, I toss my bag to the floorboard and angle my body. Not knowing if she can hear me, I lean in, pressing my cheek to the window. Cupping my hands around my mouth, I shout toward the back of the ambulance. "Meg, you can't give up now. You have too much left to tell me. You promised."

Unexpected tears stream down my face. My heart feels as though it's going to beat right out of my chest as the driver takes a sharp turn, and I see the four tall columns of the Elko hospital coming into view.

The ambulance races forward, while I plead with a woman I can't say I know, to hold on to life for a little while longer. Not for me, this time, I realize, but for Meg. She is the one who needs to be unburdened by her past. That is my only role here, and I intend to follow it through, all the way to the end.

"Hang in there, Meg. Your story isn't over yet." I will the woman I barely know to hold on.

EVERYTHING STOPS AT ONCE. The siren ceases. The lights stop their dizzying spin and the ambulance comes to an abrupt standstill at the hospital's entrance. Everything stops. Everything except my tears and anguished thoughts.

The driver turns to me. "Stay here until we've cleared the doors, then you can follow."

I acknowledge his instructions with a dip of my head,

but reposition my hand to the door's handle, ready to leap out as soon as I am able.

The hospital's emergency doors fly open as a team of doctors and nurses rush toward the back of the ambulance. A clatter of steel on steel tells me Meg's portable bed is on the move. The gaggle of crisp starched uniform-clad hospital staff surround Meg's moving cot and glide through the hospital doors with swift efficiency.

I grab my bag from the floor of the ambulance and follow them inside. Meg is wheeled past a reception area and through a set of doors that indicate no entry to me with a large red circle struck through with a bold line. The distinct aroma of a hospital surrounds me as I check in at the reception desk. I tell the woman I am with Meg and am directed to take a seat. A doctor will be with me as soon as possible.

Unable to sit, I pace the corridor, my feet moving far slower than my mind. From what I can tell, Meg doesn't have anyone else to notify, at least not that she has confided in me. Considering my options, I ask the woman at the reception desk for directions to a pay phone.

I dig out my change purse from the bottom of my bag and start dropping coins into the phone's slot. My first call is to *The Carson City News* offices. I promised my editor an update by the end of today, but with recent events, I fear I'll have little to offer until I speak with the doctor.

~

"HI, HAROLD. IT'S ME, JUNE."

"I just got off the phone with your father. He is worried about you. Says you left in a state yesterday."

"I know you mean well, but my relationship with my

father is nothing for you to worry over." I have tried over the past few months to instill a separation of work and family given my father's friendship with Harold, but so far, my efforts seem to have been in vain.

"Yes. Yes. You've said as much before. But, June, you must know how important you and your wellbeing are to your father."

"All the more reason for us to keep family dynamics out of our work life."

I hear him sigh through the phone line and feel a stab of guilt at him being put in the position of being in the middle of what my father wants.

"Anyway, I'm calling with an update. We've run into a problem here."

"What sort of problem?" Harold's voice is thick with concern.

"I'm at the hospital with Meg. She fell ill late this morning, and I had to call an ambulance."

"So, you're done with the story, then? Did you get what you need?"

I smother a moan. "Not quite."

"June, I approved your excursion to Elko with the expectation that you'd return in three days with a story in hand."

I can almost see Harold running a frustrated hand through his thinning head of hair.

"You did, but I'm not done yet and technically, I still have another day and a half plus the weekend if I wanted to take it."

"Your father is going to have my hide for this, you know. He isn't happy about the way you two left things."

"I am sorry about that." I resort to using the cheeky tone he's been familiar with since I was a child and tease. "You should choose your friends more wisely." Pausing to reassert my seriousness of the situation, I add, "Harold, this is important to me."

I can feel his resolve ebbing as I twist the telephone cord around my finger. "Important enough to give up the front-page story I promised you?"

"You have one for me?" I feel my brow furrow, knowing a tough decision is coming my way.

"I do. I said I would track one down so you could put your name on it. June, I know you didn't think so at the time, but I wasn't trying to cut your knees out from under you the last time. I was trying to protect you."

"I doubt most editors go around trying to protect their reporters." My disappointment at having my name stripped from the front-page byline has yet to subside.

"You'd be surprised." Harold's reply is dry, telling me there is more truth to his words than I could possibly imagine.

Though I'd like to take his olive branch, I can't find the enthusiasm to reach for it. Something about Meg and her story is keeping me here in Elko. I let the phone cord unravel as I consider the options before me. Meg's words ring in my ears. *Courage is seldom summoned under comfortable circumstances.*

"Harold, I can't leave. There is something here. I know it."

"I had a feeling you were going to say that. Reporter's instinct and all."

I chuckle at his understanding, certain he has heard some version of that line from every reporter who has ever worked for him.

"As long as you're sure. I have to put somebody else on the front pager. It won't wait until you return."

"I am sure, and Harold. I promise not to hold it against you."

"Alright then, Miss Monroe. Go get your story."

"Thank you. I won't let you down."

"But, June. Do me a favor and call your father. He worries about you."

"Oh, I think I see the doctor. I have to go." I have the receiver halfway to its cradle when I add, "I'll talk to you soon."

I hear Harold's muffled voice calling my name just before I hang up the phone.

The doctor, who is far younger than I would have first guessed he would be, strolls toward me. "Miss Bruno?"

"No, I mean yes. I am with Miss Bruno, but I am not Miss Bruno." I feel my cheeks flush. Extending my hand, I try again. "June Monroe."

"Ah, Miss Monroe?" The doctor dips his chin, and I sense a question in his mention of Miss.

"Yes, Miss is fine."

"Your aunt is resting now. She's had quite the morning, so rest will serve her well."

"Ah, yes. My aunt, on my mother's side." I recognize the white lie for what it is. Meg must have fibbed and told the doctor I am her niece. If I want any chance of seeing Meg within these walls, I will need to pretend to be related to her, since the family only policy is likely in place.

"When can I see her?"

"We've given her a sedative. I expect she will sleep for a few hours yet. You are welcome to wait here, or if you prefer, there is a cafeteria on the lower floor if you'd like a cup of coffee or something to eat."

"Thank you." I contemplate asking more about Meg's health but find myself unable to form the words. Whether it is out of respect for her privacy, or my fear of having to face the worst, I'm not sure.

"You can check back with the reception desk in a couple of hours. We should have an update for you by then."

My head bobs in understanding. "I appreciate it. Thank you, again."

The doctor turns and leaves, his white coat flapping in a self-made breeze. I check the time on my watch and head to the cafeteria.

Twenty-Eight

MEG

THE OVERHEAD LIGHTS ARE DIMMED, BUT THE continual bustling beyond the half-open door is enough to ensure the weary will not be rewarded with a restful sleep. There is no clock in the room. If I had to guess, I'd say it's close to four o'clock, given the light coming through the small window at the far end of the dreary room.

I was startled awake from a fitful sleep, unsure of where I was at first. A rush of emotion brought it all back. Reality is difficult to hide from when it forces its way into your line of sight. I've known it for a while now, but even the doctor's letter did little to make the news sink in completely.

I am dying.

The brittle starched sheets imprison my body like a straitjacket. Intended, I presume, to offer a layer of comfort, their hospital corners elicit only panic within me. I shift my legs back and forth. Up and down. Doing all I can to release the fenced in sheets free of their folds. I despise the sensation of feeling trapped. I can't imagine anyone appreciating being tucked in tight, with or without the familiarity of an extended jail term. Forced to remain on my back, given the narrow nature of the bed, I am distressed. A fresh wave of alarm grips my chest as the memory spirals around me.

Twenty-Nine

NOVEMBER 1925
ELKO, NEVADA

MEG

THE STALE AIR SWIRLS, ENCIRCLING MY BODY WITH the eerie swish of a wintery gust. Over the past two and a half years, my comfort within the tunnels has yet to show itself. George assured me I'd get used to the sensation of being underground. He told me the more often I used the tunnels, the less troubled I'd become. George was wrong.

Despite weekly trips through the cavernous and dirty hollowed-out earth to transport crates of liquor between George's warehouse and Bootlegger's Bluff, I still look over my shoulder. Peering into the darkness with only a flashlight for guidance, I can't shake the feeling of danger lurking among the shadows.

I pull the wagon behind me, thankful the four wheeled device is at least useful in reducing the number of trips and thus the time I must spend traipsing back and forth with bootlegged liquor. With my stock list clutched in my damp palm, I round the corner and walk straight into a spiderweb.

The wagon's handle drops with a thump to the dirt floor as I swat the sticky web away from my face. I hold back the scream that is ready to launch, move to the side of the wagon, and take three large steps backward.

Muttering profanities sure to make a sailor blush, I gather myself before examining the space in front of me under the light of the flashlight's beam. Taking tentative steps, I reassure myself with the knowledge that George's warehouse is a short distance away. Two more turns and the door that leads to the ladder is in front of me.

I rest the wagon's handle against the tunnel wall and position my flashlight within the wagon's bed so its beam shines toward the door and access point to the warehouse. I use my shoulder to lean into the heavy wood door with a hefty shove, thankful for the physical strength that comes with a bootlegging lifestyle. Having shifted from years of settlement, the door groans its displeasure as the bottom edge carves out a deep rut of caked dirt from its path. I press my full body weight against the door, wedging it into an open position, and turn my attention to the makeshift ladder in front of me.

Placing a hand on a ladder rung, I heave my body up and my foot lands on the first rail—hand over hand. I am halfway up the ten-rung ladder when a frightening creak yanks my attention back. The door, slow at first, quickly gathers speed and slams shut, descending me into pitch black darkness.

An icy chill snakes down my spine, though I can't tell if it is from dread or actually dropping temperatures. My eyes adjust slowly to the darkness. Up or down? I consider my options. Deciding up offers the most hope of assistance given the missing door handle on this side of the tunnel door, I fumble the five remaining steps toward the trapdoor. Counting the rungs as I go, I clamp my lips shut to stop me from hollering. I've no intention of looking the fool in front of the boys and screeching like a banshee is a sure way to undermine any strides I've made in becoming respected among them.

My head bumps against the trapdoor first, before my hands feel the slats of the wood planks. Relief rushes through me as my fingers find the round metal handle. I pull the handle while thrusting my shoulder against the trapdoor. My force defies me and instead of granting me access to George's warehouse, it causes me to stumble and almost lose my footing on the ladder.

Bracing myself, I curve my back against the rugged and narrow shaft where the ladder sits, and try again. All I can think is, the below zero temperatures must have caused the wood to shift as the door into George's warehouse remains firmly sealed. Panic wastes no time and before I can reel it back, I am hammering on the underside of the trapdoor with everything I have.

Images of being left to die slowly in the frigid shaft between George's warehouse and the tunnel grow more vivid by the minute.

How long would it take them to find me?

The thought of never seeing George again spurs me into a frenzy, and I holler and shriek with utter desperation.

Several minutes later, my voice is hoarse from screaming and my body aches. I am drenched in sweat and chilled to the bone as the unsettling realization stares back at me. The warehouse must be empty, and I am trapped.

Thirty

AUGUST 1955
ELKO, NEVADA

MEG

MY LEG KICKS FREE OF THE STARCHED LINENS, jerking me free from my remembered nightmare. My agitation probably has more to do with my impending demise than it does with the hospital bedding, but I am not in the mood to shine a light on my emotional state at the moment. I do my best to calm myself, forcing my mind to think back over the events of the morning as my hands busy themselves by folding and unfolding the scratchy linen tucked tight against my chest. The repetitive action soothes me some, slowing my breaths to a less frantic state.

Breakfast with June this morning was pleasant as we soaked up the early morning rays on the front porch. I was quite pleased with myself for talking candidly about George. A step in the right direction, if I do say so myself. I even enjoyed a few sips of real coffee, something I haven't been able to stomach since the cancer started stealing even the tiniest of pleasures from me several months ago. My lungs never fully recovered from the time I spent in jail. Even now, I wonder if the pneumonia I endured there was the beginning of my end.

A weary sigh deflates my whole being at the awareness of how far there is to go before June and I share the same understanding of the events of the raid that landed me in jail. There is no turning back for me now. The girl must know the truth. It is the least I can do for her, given the circumstances.

I consider the girl's determination. In all honesty, I want to see June succeed. I sense the fire in her belly stems from wanting to become someone who makes a difference in other's lives. She may tout a good line about seeking fame as a reporter, but something tells me it is the desire to make things right in the world that truly propels her forward. I imagine her mother is proud of her.

Images of my parents drift through my memory, bringing with them regret as wide as the Grand Canyon. A silver lining exists. My Catholic upbringing instilled in me the possibility of seeing them again in heaven. I will repent the entirety of my life here on earth if only I will be afforded the luxury to beg their forgiveness of me face to face in the afterlife.

I look up, startling when I see June standing in the doorway. The girl is watching me with an expression riddled with contradiction. Worry and expectation mix together, adding to her youthful appearance. My biggest wish is that she can handle what I am about to confess.

"I said I would tell you my story. I am prepared to do so now."

"Come in. Please have a seat." I gesture to the chair near the side of the bed before tugging the thin sheet back up to my chest, not wishing to scare the girl with my state of hospital undress.

"I didn't mean to disturb you." June takes a hesitant step into the room. "If you'd rather rest, I can come back later."

The girl is sweet. I offer her what I expect is a melancholy smile. "I'm afraid later is no longer a guarantee where I am concerned."

June drags the uncomfortable-looking chair closer to my bedside. Placing her bag on the floor, she takes in the room with a sweep of her eyes. I try to imagine how it all looks from her perspective, but I can't focus on anything besides the task before me.

"How are you feeling?" June leans in, tilting her head to look me in the eye.

"Much better. Now that the coughing has subsided."

"You gave me quite the scare." June's gaze falls to her lap. "I didn't realize you were ill. I am sorry about that."

"Yes, well. We don't really know one another, do we?" My fingers return to working the stitched edge of the stiff sheet. I imagine the girl wants to ask what ails me, but politeness overrules her impulse, reporter or not.

"I wanted to thank you—" My parched throat does little for a smooth delivery of words.

June interjects before I can finish my thought. "Of course. Anyone would have telephoned for help."

"I—I meant to say thank you for asking them to call me Miss instead of Mrs. It was kind of you to remember that."

The pink blush creeps up June's neck, licking its way past her ears, all the way to her forehead. Though I try to, I cannot suppress a smile. The familiarity of her physical reaction to being embarrassed transports me back in time without hesitation.

Glancing over the bed's rail, I take in the same coloring, arriving like a spilled can of paint, onto her hands and up her arms. There were other similarities, of course, but this one takes the cake, and I know for certain my time spent researching if this girl is the right June Monroe has not been in vain.

"Would you like some water?" The girl stands and pours from the pitcher without waiting for my response. Pulling a lever, she eases the bed and my torso to sitting. "That's better."

Adding a straw to the cup, June hands it to me and I sip.

"Thank you." The hoarseness of my voice relaxes with the infusion of moisture.

The girl returns to her chair, her lips twisting as she considers her words. "You mentioned something earlier that has got me curious. What did you mean when you said I deserved to know the truth?"

I rest the cup in my lap and meet June's eyes. Taking as deep a breath as my worn out lungs will allow, I draw out the exhalation and ready myself. The time to tell all the truth has arrived. "You wanted to know about my life and the trial."

June's head bobs once.

"I assume it was because you suspected something wasn't as it seemed."

Another silent nod.

"I don't know how you came to surmise this from a few aged newspaper articles, but I can confirm, you are not wrong."

The girl sits taller in her chair. A faint smile graces her lips. I imagine her quelling the desire to shout *I knew it* to the entire hospital.

"You might want to get your notebook out for this." I incline my head toward her bag on the floor.

June pulls out her notebook and pencil, flipping the book open to a clean page.

I mull the order of the delivery of information in my head, contemplating the clearest path to understanding. "The raid was legitimate enough."

"Ah, we are awake, I see." A nurse I don't recall having met strides into the room with a high-pitched edge to her singsong voice.

Both our heads swivel in her direction.

"Well, Miss Bruno, the doctor has ordered some tests."

I can't fathom why anyone would bother with more tests given my state. Managing the symptoms is all that can be done, according to the letter I received from my doctor's office. I didn't even return as requested by the office for another appointment. If nothing can be done, I am less than inclined to waste my time seeing doctors and having tests done.

"No." With all the information present and accounted for, my answer is obvious. How much time I have left is not guaranteed. I have no desire to spend it having tests done when I should be focused on telling June everything she deserves to know.

The nurse bends her elbows, placing a fist on either side of both hips. She narrows her eyes and pinches her lips together in displeasure. "No, isn't an option, Miss Bruno. The doctor sets the rules around here and you are scheduled for tests." She finishes her declaration with a false, though acutely assured, tight smile.

June stands. "Maybe I should go. We want to make sure you get the best treatment, Meg." Moving closer to the bed,

June squeezes her hand in mine, leaning in with her voice slightly above a whisper. "We don't want anyone to get off on the wrong foot here, especially when they"—she quirks her head sideways in the nurse's direction—"are in charge of visitation."

I tuck out of sight the scornful look I'd like to toss the nurse, and instead agree with a vague nod in June's direction.

"Do what they ask of you, and I'll come back later."

"Good. Good." The nurse resumes her high-spirited communication as June gives me a reassuring little wave from the door.

Thirty-One

JUNE

"Now, Miss Bruno, we need to get you up and moving a bit." The nurse's commanding cheerfulness bounces into the hallway with me. I stifle a smirk, more than aware Meg is likely gritting her teeth at the woman.

The hospital's odor of cleaning products mixed with hot food makes my nose wrinkle as I stroll down the corridor with no destination in mind. Checking my watch, I note the dinner hour, which explains the aroma filling the hall. Harold's insistent voice rings in my head. "Call your father."

No time like the present.

I make my way toward the pay phone in the hospital lobby. My father is many things but late for dinner is not one of them. I am quite sure I'll be interrupting their meal with my telephone call. My mother is probably setting the carrots and peas in the crockery at this very moment.

Then again, I tap a finger against my bottom lip. A telephone call cut short due to dinner cooling on the table may be just the thing to excuse me from a lengthy dressing down by my father. With that in mind, I plunk a few coins into the slot and wait for the connection to ring through.

"Monroe residence." My mother's delighted greeting gives no indication she is in the middle of anything. Instead, it sounds as if she's simply been standing by the telephone waiting for it to ring.

"Hi, Mom, it's me."

"June, dear. Is everything alright? We are just about to sit down to dinner."

I can hear my mother's almost imperceptible tsk as my father in the background asks who is on the phone.

"I won't keep you from your dinner. Everything is fine. I wanted to let you know I won't be coming home tomorrow. I need to stay a few extra days to finish up."

"Oh, I see." My mother's voice trails off, and I imagine her looking at my father, knowing she will be the one to break the news to him.

"Who is it, Helen?" His voice is gruff but that could mean anything from tired to worried to angry. I've given up trying to discern which of his emotions is being directed at me and, more often than not, assume it is disappointment in some form or fashion.

"Just a minute, dear." What I suspect is my mother's hand covering the mouthpiece, muffles through the telephone wires.

"Let me speak to her." The hairs on the back of my neck rise when I hear my father's voice followed by the kerfuffle of the handset changing hands.

"June, you are worrying your mother by running off like you did. You are to come home at once."

"Dad, you don't understand." I try to reason with him

despite knowing our most recent argument is likely what is fueling his continued irritation with me.

"When you come home, we can sit down and discuss it like adults. But for now, you are my daughter and—"

"Dad." My voice is almost at shouting level when a quick glance around the brightly lit, but still drab hospital lobby, reminds me of where I am. "I am doing my job. Harold knows I've been delayed and not that it matters, but he is fine with it."

I can almost see him standing there, shaking his head at my willful nature.

"Need I remind you that you have your mother's car?"

I sink my teeth into my bottom lip to hold back the cuss word that is eager to fly. I forgot about the car. I left it at Meg's house, choosing to hop in the ambulance instead.

My mother's voice is agreeable in the background, but insistent all the same. "Albert, I've no plans to go anywhere. The car is fine with June as long as she is all right."

My father clears his throat, a sure sign he is unwilling to concede the point.

"Dad, I wasn't due back until tomorrow evening, anyway." I do my best to nudge the defiance from my words, keeping my voice level. "I'm sorry about the car. If it is alright with Mom, I promise to be back as soon as I can."

Undeterred, he tries another tactic. "You weren't scheduled to go away." Silence fills the distance between us, and I assume he is attempting to curb his irritation with me. "Harold mentioned he had a story for you. Surely, you'll listen to your editor." I can hear the assuredness in his voice. He thinks he's got me.

I run my fingers through my hair while turning my back

on the hospital reception desk and the woman whose eyebrows are creeping higher toward her hairline with each escalation of my voice. "I've passed on the other story."

"I see." His condescending tone is coated with righteousness. "So, it isn't true. You aren't actually seeking a career in journalism then. You are just roaming about the country on whatever whim crosses your path."

I am about to refute him when he bulldozes me with further reprimands.

"You are to come home immediately. Do you hear me?"

Meg's promise to tell me her story presses in on me. My head thrums with my father's words battling against my belief that there is something here. I know it in my heart. Meg's story is important. I just can't explain the reason I'm convinced of it. Trying to do so now will only make me appear more unhinged than I did walking out the door of my family home in the middle of an argument.

"Daddy, I love you, but I'm not coming home until I've finished what I set out to do."

Without waiting for his reply, I hang up the telephone. Pride over having stood up to my father mixes with dread at how I've likely hurt him as I distance myself from the telephone. The emotion is quick to arrive and tears prick my eyes as I retrace my path through the hospital corridors toward Meg's room.

~

SELF-DOUBT IS A RELIABLE COMPANION. Especially when my father's words make it so easy for me to question the validity of my own thoughts. Isn't it enough that he instilled his values in me as a small child? Does he genuinely think I could stray so far from who he knows me to be that I'd be unredeemable?

"Honest to goodness." The words sigh out of me.

I peek my head into Meg's room, but her bed is empty. Taking another lap around the hospital, I mull over what is sure to be a challenging conversation when I return home. Perhaps it's time for me to consider an apartment of my own. My father won't be pleased, but then again, I am not pleasing him much now anyway. If I move out, at least I won't constantly be in his line of fire. I tuck the thought to the back of my mind and determine to revisit the topic on my drive home from Elko.

A vending machine draws my attention at the end of the corridor. Nestled into a cubby with a cluster of wood benches a short few steps away, the waiting room looks less than inviting. I consider another visit to the cafeteria but decide better of it, knowing the offering of the same egg salad sandwich I had for lunch has likely gotten no better in the time that has passed since I ventured there for lunch a few hours ago.

Dropping a nickel into the vending machine, I grab the soda and keep on walking. A restless mind is often eased by a moving body, or so my mother likes to say. I sip from my soda, the fizzy mixture coating my tongue in a sweet sensation.

Seeking a different view than the repetitive, drab walls of the hospital corridor, I climb the stairs to the next floor. The muffled silence of the stairwell is a welcomed relief given the beeping, buzzing, and whispering that goes on throughout the rest of the building.

An hour later, after scanning every magazine the hospital

waiting room has to offer, I head back to Meg's room, hopeful of finding her waiting and ready for me. Having been unsuccessful at steering my mind away from the tense conversation with my father, I am more than eager to hear what Meg has to say, if only to remind me of my purpose here.

The door to Meg's room is almost closed. I tap on the oversized door with a light knock. With no reply coming from within, I push the door open an inch. "Meg?"

Seeing Meg settled in her hospital bed, deep in sleep, has me pausing in the middle of the threshold. My plans to continue our conversation are once again thwarted.

I feel a presence behind me and turn to find the boisterous nurse with a finger to her lips. She gestures me out into the hallway and closes Meg's door behind us.

"I'm sorry dear, she's going to be out for the night." Though she is delivering apologies, I am almost certain she isn't even the slightest bit sorry.

"Maybe I should stay, just in case." I glance back over my shoulder toward the closed door. "I know Meg wants me to stay. She doesn't have anyone else." As I plead my case, I feel the hitch of emotion in my throat. Meg doesn't have anyone else but me.

"You best go on home. Get some rest yourself." The nurse places a firm hand on my back, guiding me toward the lobby and the main exit of the building.

When I hesitate for a second, she adds. "We've given her a sedative. She won't wake until morning." The nurse's encouraging nod leaves little room to argue.

"Oh, alright then." It feels wrong to leave Meg now, but how can I argue as I'm being escorted to the door?

I give my motel's name and phone number to the nurse

at the reception desk and step through the hospital doors into the dry Nevada air.

The parking lot, with only a handful of cars remaining, greets me, and I am reminded once again that my mother's car is still parked at Meg's house.

Thirty-Two

MEG

THE WINTER WIND TEARS THROUGH MY FUR-trimmed overcoat, eliciting a full body shiver as I round the corner toward George's stock warehouse. Jutting my chin, I take in the gray skies from beneath my wool-lined beret. The cold weather hat, another gift from George, is doing little to ward off the frigid temperatures that have been threatening snow for days.

I wouldn't even be out here this afternoon. Staying tucked up in my apartment for another day with a cup of tea and the latest crime fiction novel seemed far more sensible. I fear I am getting too old for this racket, but George, continually needing to know every dime accumulated from a week-end's distribution, insisted I check the inventory and tally the accounts.

The task, part of my usual Monday morning routine, was delayed by yesterday's frosty weather. I watched from my apartment window as the few cars that ventured out were sent slipping and sliding through town as if they were ice skating on the frozen pond.

Tucking my chin deeper into the soft fur, I hurry my steps, eager to be free of the cold and the risk of being spotted near the warehouse. Since most Elko residents are hunkered down inside, given the many downtown businesses that remain closed because of the inclement weather, I must be careful as a lone female wandering around the buildings near the train tracks could easily be deemed suspicious.

With temperatures well below freezing, I am determined not to traipse through the underground tunnels on my own today, or ever again, if I have anything to say about it. The tunnels have continued to make my skin crawl no matter how many times I'd navigated them over the years. With last November's incident still fresh in my mind, and still haunting my nightmares, I will avoid the tunnels for as long as I can.

I shudder at the thought of the ordeal. I spent the better part of three hours trapped in the claustrophobic and musty shaft where the ladder to George's warehouse was located. Imprisoned between a wedged shut door and an inoperable trapdoor, I was left to ponder my demise between bouts of hollering for help. I only discovered, upon being rescued, that the trapdoor was inoperable because one of the boys inadvertently rolled a wine barrel over top of one side of it. No, my wariness when it comes to the safety of the secret route through the tunnels is more than warranted. The thought of being trapped down there in the middle of a winter storm is enough to have me brave this riskier option today.

I wore my most drab coat, hoping to blend in with the

dark wood of the weathered structure of the warehouse. The color did little to conceal me as I moved about the downtown corridor, but now, with George's warehouse in sight, I can see how easily I will disappear against the building as I work the lock to gain entrance.

Pressing my back to the side of the building, I take careful steps toward the rear, where the single door is partially hidden by an unruly sage brush. My gloved fingers clasp the padlock as I lean in to ensure the lock itself hasn't been changed. Reaching into my pocket, I pull out the key George gave me for safekeeping. Though I am certain he didn't expect I would ever use the key, I am grateful he is steadfast with having a slew of backup plans.

I take a last glance around and, hearing no one, I slide the lock from the door and slip stealthily inside. The cool, musty air assaults my nostrils like a hammer to a nail, and I cover my nose with the back of my gloved hand.

I squeeze past a tower of unopened crates, making a mental note to remind George to have the hay bales he uses to disguise the scent of alcohol swapped out if he doesn't want his stash inadvertently discovered by a copper with a big nose. Though the warehouse is, for the most part, away from prying eyes, with the feds scouring every inch of Nevada for those profiting from Prohibition, one can never be too careful.

My breath billows ahead of me in puffs of clouds as I walk with quick steps to the small office. It's a good thing alcohol is far more resistant to freezing than water, given the warehouse's lack of heat. Sliding the gloves off my fingers, I remove the account ledger from behind a false wall panel that creates an imperceptible storage space just large enough to hide George's important documents.

Settling in front of the makeshift desk, I get straight to work.

If I didn't need to keep my wits about me, I might consider imbibing in a shot of whiskey to chase the chill away. But mixing liquor with numbers has never been an option for me, especially when the numbers are crucial to the success of an operation such as ours.

The hours pass like minutes while my toes disappear into numbness within my tall lace-up boots, despite the layer of sheep's wool lining the inside. In contrast, my fingers, pinched tight around my pencil, are impervious to the cold so long as my focus remains on the ledger in front of me.

A shuffle of movement perks my ears to attention. I sit, still as a statue, not daring to breathe, much less move. I could be imagining things or it might be a rodent in search of a slice of shelter from the cold. Either way, waiting the disturbance out is my only option. Knowing that George and the boys continued on with their plans for the day despite the foul weather, my awareness remains tuned in to every whisper of sound.

Several minutes pass in silence. I am about to breathe a sigh of relief when something or someone knocks up against the outside wall opposite where I sit, rendering me immobile. The hairs on the back of my neck rise, informing me that something is amiss.

I place the pencil on top of the desk without a sound. Pulling my coat sleeve up a fraction, I steal a quick glance at my wristwatch. I note the time. Three-fifteen. Not nearly late enough for the boys to be returning. I had planned on remaining in place at the warehouse until the cover of darkness could aid my return home.

Another rattle, this time from the front of the building.

Definitely not an animal, I surmise as a jolt of panic raises my heartbeat. It could be kids, kept home from school because of the impending storm and left to run amok. A rattle and a bang cause me to jump, almost out of my skin. Cursing silently, I still myself and scan every inch of the warehouse I can see from my vantage point.

I pinpoint the origin of the sound and focus my attention there. The front warehouse sliding door has a chain and a padlock securing it in place. Someone is toying with the lock, causing the chain to bang against the oversized sliding wood door. Within the warehouse, the sound echoes against the hard surfaces, reverberating around the crates and barrels like a shotgun during target practice.

Whether it's foreshadowing or plain bad luck, I can't decide. I am contemplating my options when a single gunshot rings out, splitting the air with its reverberation. Instinct takes over, forcing me to take cover beneath the desk while protecting my head with my arms.

The shot is followed by the rattle of the chain being pulled through the door's metal handles. I am spurred into action. Having heard the stories while keeping a keen eye on local newspaper reports, I know without a doubt, this is a raid. George's warehouse has been discovered and his current stash of hundreds of gallons of liquor is about to be discovered.

Not wasting another minute, I snag the pencil and ledger from the desk and crab walk my way toward the false paneled wall, doing my best to remain hidden should the warehouse doors fly open and expose me. They may nab us with the warehouse's current inventory, but I'll be damned if I'm the one responsible for providing the dry agents with the map to George's web of businesses.

Forcing the false panel back in place, I scan the room for evidence of anything that might indicate the heart of the operation lives here. Seeing nothing, I pivot and step as far away from the office as I can, determined to put as much space as possible between me and the documents that could send George away for a very long time.

"George," I whisper as I glance toward the trapdoor.

Protect the tribe, Maria, and then protect the merchandise. His words echo in the back corner of my mind. There is little hope of protecting the merchandise today, but George —I hesitate. Can I protect him?

With the access to the tunnels hidden in plain sight, I question if I could make it in time without being discovered. There are no barrels blocking my path today. All I have to do is wedge a finger into the knot in the wood and slip out of sight and down the ladder to freedom.

The thought of descending into the depths below, without knowing if George is out of harm's way, paralyzes me. The sound of metal scraping against metal summons a dread so deep it feels pulled from my soul. I am out of time.

When the door is breached, I am standing in the middle of the warehouse surrounded by barrels and crates of Brunelli sacramental wine. Though the labels have been stripped from the bottles and the barrels are nondescript, the irony of once again being caught red-handed with my father's wine is not lost on me. Several men, dressed in dark overcoats and tweed hats, storm through the sliding door, bringing the bitter air with them as they seek their reward.

Some carry crowbars, others hammers, and the one in the lead, a shotgun. But all of them stop in their tracks when their eyes fall on me. The man with the shotgun tilts his head in question, surprise showing in his raised eyebrows, before sliding the gun to his back and away from my line of sight.

"Ma'am?" He lifts his hat in greeting, and for a split second, I think he might simply let me walk away.

A whip of wind sends a biting chill all the way through me and my body shudders in response.

I am so cold.

The hard reality of my situation fills me with panic.

Thirty-Three

AUGUST 1955

ELKO, NEVADA

MEG

THE SHIVER RUNS THROUGH ME, RATTLING MY frail body. "So cold. So cold." I hear the words on repeat, though they sound as if they are coming from someone else much farther away.

Frantic fingers, gnarled in on themselves, clench the blankets tighter, desperate to feel the reprieve of warmth. "No. Please. You can't take me." A sob escapes, burning my throat and waking me from the nightmare.

Tears make haste down my face, my bed's elevated position aiding in their trajectory. My eyes, now open, dart around the shadowy room as if danger is lurking in the corners.

A sliver of light expands as a door creaks open into the room. A young woman in a white uniform and cap is at my side in two strides. "Miss Bruno, is everything alright?"

Recognition dawns on me. I am in the hospital. "Cold."

CHAPTER THIRTY-THREE

My teeth chatter as I utter the only word that holds any importance.

Retrieving another blanket from a cabinet, the nurse covers my body before tucking the blanket loosely around my shoulders. "Is that better?"

I nod my head, thankful she has not pinned me down with the thing.

Moving to the foot of my bed, the nurse picks up a clipboard and reads it through. Returning to my side of the bed, she places a warm, comforting hand on my shoulder. "It seems you were given a sedative to help you sleep. Sometimes, when a patient wakes up from it abruptly, things feel a bit out of sorts. Not to worry, Miss Bruno, you'll be feeling much more yourself soon."

The nurse bustles around me, checking my pulse, then my temperature. When she seems convinced that I am, in fact, fine, she gives my shoulder another squeeze. "It's not quite three o'clock yet. Why don't you try to go back to sleep now? I'm sure you'll feel much better when you wake a little later in the morning."

With a firm nod of her head, she walks out, closing the door behind her.

Left alone in the room, I have little option but to sleep once more. Still groggy, my eyes close of their own accord.

It feels as though only minutes have passed when my eyes fly open again as a fresh vibration of bone-numbing cold ripples through me. The sensation feels acutely real as vivid memories of me standing, for what seemed like hours, in the frigid winter air while Prohibition agents decided my fate, fill me with a heavy weight of foreboding.

"I'll never be warm again." The words slip from my cracked

lips in a whisper. All of my memories of that day and the subsequent days, weeks, and months in jail that followed are tied to a deep-seated fear of being unable to feel warm again. Instinctively, I reach to pull my sweater, my daily assurance that all will be well, tighter around my shoulders, but find it missing.

My heart sinks at the realization. Perhaps all will not be well, ever again. Caught somewhere between sleep and awake, with teeth chattering and cold coursing through me as waves of emotion assault me, all I can think is I've missed my chance for redemption. I hesitated again, and I am going to have to die with the consequences.

Thirty-Four

JUNE

MEG'S HOUSE IS DARK AS NIGHT WHEN THE TAXI cab pulls away from the curb. The slow rising moon offers a slim shimmer of light as I drop my bag onto the front seat of my mother's station wagon and contemplate my next move. My thoughts reel back to the events of this morning. I was the last to leave the house, and with Meg incapacitated, I am certain the cat is either trapped inside or out, though I can't recall which.

I am Meg's sole point of contact, as far as I'm aware, so my head drops with the knowledge of what I must do. I push myself forward and climb Meg's front porch steps.

Normally, I would never consider allowing myself into someone else's home without their permission. I wish I had had the foresight to discuss this plan with Meg when a soft meow draws my attention.

"Kitty." I bend to address the black cat. His position

sitting close on my heels tells me he is both hungry and tired of being outdoors all day. "Let's get you something to eat, then."

Meg's unlocked door opens without hesitation as the cat dashes past me toward the kitchen. I flip on the light closest to the door and follow the cat, assuming he knows where the food is kept. As expected, Kitty is purring with reckless abandon while circling back and forth in front of a low cupboard. I scan the room and find a water and food dish tucked into the corner at the end of a run of cabinets.

Refilling the water dish at the tap, I let my gaze roam the kitchen. Meg's house is tidy, something I had paid little attention to earlier. I return the cat's water dish to what I assume is its usual place and open the cupboard Kitty was none too shy about pointing out to me. "You were right." I give the cat's head a quick scratch and retrieve the bag of kibble.

The cat food cascades from the bag, making a raucous clattering sound as it hits the empty bowl. I fill it to the brim, uncertain of how much or how often Kitty will get to eat in the coming days. The cat sets straight to work, allowing me the time to figure out my next course of action.

I consider Meg at the hospital without any of her necessities from home. I imagine she could use a toothbrush, hairbrush, and maybe a sweater to put on over that awful hospital gown they've made her wear. Surely, the sweater and clothes she went to the hospital in are there somewhere with her, but given the brusqueness I've experienced from the nurses so far, I'm not convinced finding them will be an easy task.

How upset will she be knowing I've been through her things, even if it is for her benefit? I weigh the options and decide that if it were me, I'd want a few comforts from home to make a hospital stay a little easier.

I open cupboard doors until I find a paper bag from the local grocer. With Kitty still content at his bowl, I take tentative steps toward the back of the house. In the bathroom, I find a toothbrush and paste, a hairbrush, and a jar of hand cream that, given its prominent placement on the counter, seems to be important to Meg. I tuck all the items into the bag and move on to her bedroom.

A double bed and a chest of drawers takes up most of the room. My gaze falls on a grouping of photographs on top of the dresser. I step closer, curiosity getting the better of me. A younger Meg stares back at me, the camera having caught her mid-laugh, lifts my own lips into a smile. A family of four is next, and I lean forward, eager to gain a sense of who they were. Perhaps it is the era of the photographs, but they seem familiar to me.

I shrug off the thought, aware that black-and-white photos can have a slight resemblance to one another due to the technology of the time. Even my Grandma Ruth's photo album needed her deciphering knowledge to tell one relative apart from another.

I find one of Meg's sweaters on the back of her bedroom door, thankful for the awareness that Meg will know I did not rifle through her things and only brought what is useful and readily available.

With everything gathered, I check on Kitty. He has curled himself into a ball on the sofa, and I assume that is where he will stay for the night. I'm about to leave when I think of grabbing Meg's house keys to lock the door behind me.

Returning to the kitchen, I spot the keys in a dish on the

table. A letter, folded on top of the dish, draws my attention with its crinkled edges from what I presume is frequent reading. I inch closer, unable to stop. I can feel it in the pit of my stomach. This letter will tell me what I need to know about Meg. I push down the impropriety of reading another's correspondence.

If I'm to do right by Meg, I need to know what I'm dealing with. Before I can talk myself out of it, I reach my fingers forward and snatch the letter from the dish.

April 12, 1955

Dear Miss Bruno,

I regret to inform you that your condition is as we feared. I had hoped to speak with you directly on the matter, but you did not return for our previously scheduled follow up appointment and my office has been unable to reach you by telephone.

In light of this, I am confirming the diagnosis of lung cancer via this correspondence. I strongly encourage you to telephone our offices and schedule an appointment immediately. Please reach out to me directly with any questions you may have.

Sincerely,

Dr. Timothy Jones

The paper bag holding Meg's comforts from home drops to the linoleum floor. I barely have time to pull the kitchen chair out to catch me when I slump into it.

Meg has cancer!

The news slices through me as my mind rewinds through the conversations we've shared over the past two days. Her offhanded comments. The lack of appetite. Her desire to tell me her story and the fear that holds her back from doing so. The coughing fit that sent her to the hospital. I understand what she meant now by saying her time is short.

How short? Too short for us to finish our interview?

I admonish myself at the thought of worrying over the interview. That is the last thing Meg should be concerned about. A slow sigh whistles through my lips. The only thing I can do for her now is help her be as comfortable as possible. Shaking the sorrow I'm not certain I have a right to from my existence, I stand, pushing in the chair and grabbing the bag. First things first. I'll drop Meg's things back at the hospital before heading to the motel.

EXHAUSTED from the past two days and the news of Meg's diagnosis, I return to the motel in a daze. Dropping my bag onto the chair in the corner of my room, the statement twists through my brain on repeat.

Meg has cancer.

I can't decide whether it's the discovery that has my head spinning, or that, according to the doctor's letter, Meg has known for months. She didn't say a word about her condition in the two days I've spent with her. If I had to guess, I'd say she not only didn't bring her diagnosis up in conversation, but she may also have been downplaying her symptoms, for her, or perhaps for my benefit.

She doesn't owe me anything. I know this to be true. But, given the reason for my trip to Elko, I would have thought she would at the very least say something to indicate her situation. I slump onto the bed, my head finding comfort within my hands with the day's events.

What now? Despite the fatigue cloaking my body, my mind is far too busy to entertain the idea of sleep. I try again to get a handle on what has happened and what I plan to do in response. I have no way of knowing if Meg will be able to finish the interview. Not that it has been much of an interview, if I'm being honest. In reality, our time together has been dictated by Meg. She is the one determining when and what gets said. But before being rushed to the hospital, she did say she would tell me the whole story. In her moment of desperation, she even begged me to stay. Surely that counts for something.

A bubble of distress over the woman's prognosis rises in my chest. Is this Meg's last ditch effort to tell her side of things? Something deep inside me wants to help her do just that. But without fail, my thoughts shift to the involvement I have in Meg telling her story. I can't untangle any mention of Meg's story from the things I will personally gain by having written it. Guilt over my concern when it comes to the interview mixes as well as oil in water when the very next thought to consume me is how such a front-page article will ease the advancement of my career. Nothing about my awareness sits well when viewed through the lens of Meg's cancer.

Frustration pushes me from the bed and sets me to pacing across the dull brown carpet, my pedal pushers rustling with each anguished step. I gave up a guaranteed front-page story earlier today. One Harold was literally going to drop in my lap. I told him no, with barely a hint of hesitation. He didn't even have the chance to tell me what the front-page news article was about. I was that convinced of the importance of my remaining in Elko.

Then why do I feel as though the ground is quaking beneath me like a Nevada earthquake? I fall onto the bed, stomach first, the scent of freshly laundered bedding filling my nose. Deflated by a ruminating mind with no end in sight, I lay motionless as my mind works to sort out the problem.

Several minutes later, it occurs to me that all of my decisions were made prior to learning about Meg being diagnosed with cancer. I roll onto my back and pull myself to sitting. The letter from the doctor shouldn't change anything.

"But it does." The words whisper from my lips, along with the reality of the situation. For reasons I have no justification for, I'm scared. For Meg, for me, for the story that is sure to set her free. I am worried we're too late. Meg said she didn't want to disappoint me, yet I find myself dangerously close to being the one disappointing her.

No. I won't give up.

The only thing to do is to stay the course. Meg promised she would tell me the rest of the story. All I can do is trust that she will be true to her word and pray there is enough time left for her to do just that. This is going to be much more difficult than anything I could have imagined when I first set out for Elko. I hadn't counted on my emotions getting in the way, after all.

I move to the desk and pull out a fresh sheet of paper, determined to record today's events and information. If I'm all Meg has, then I better be prepared to show her I'm willing to go the distance for her story.

Thirty-Five

MEG

MY BODY JERKS AWAKE WITH A START. A QUICK gasp of air turns into a fierce coughing fit without hesitation. Unable to catch my breath, I grip the bed's side rails and brace myself against the rattling hack that is sure to shake my teeth loose. The cough is getting worse and yet it is far from being my first concern.

A fitful night of sleep has left my mind weary and my body tired. As the cough subsides, it leaves me with a wheezing breath that, for once, sounds far worse than it feels. Falling back onto the pillow, I loll my head toward the small window. The sun is finally rising, its orange glow casting a ray of warmth around the window's frame. That is something to be grateful for. Another day is upon us— another chance to tell June the truth.

Despite my sleepless night, I woke with a renewed determination to come clean with June. I've let too much time pass. Wasted hours when I should have been entrusting the girl with my past. Pride has a habit of getting in my way. Well, pride and stubbornness, I suppose.

I have been afraid to speak the words. Saying such things out loud is sure to make them feel even more true. Even more real. I've spent a lifetime avoiding difficult conversations, for fear of being hurt. Or worse, for fear of being rejected. What I didn't realize is, being unwilling to bare my soul results in the inability for anyone else to truly know who I am.

Oddly, this somehow didn't protect me from being hurt or rejected. Instead, I found myself hurt in other ways. I learned this lesson the hard way. Knowing this now, though, doesn't make it any easier to overcome having been taken advantage of. I put my faith in the wrong people, and I was rejected by all those who meant the most to me. But, the worst of it isn't the outright rejection, instead it's that I've been unable to move forward and trust a single person since then. That is the true misfortune of it all. George and my brother didn't only steal from me in the moment, they stole my future too.

Wasted time indeed—that ends today. I feel a surge of confidence growing within me once more. Today, I will tell June everything.

My spirits lift as the door to my hospital room whooshes open. June. I almost call her name out, my desire to see the girl at the forefront of my mind.

"Good morning, Miss Bruno." The pleasant nurse from last night sweeps into the room carrying a tray. "I have some breakfast for you."

My heart sinks at the sight of her. She is friendly enough and has a better bedside manner than the one resembling a general in the army, but the young nurse isn't who I was hoping to see.

"Thank you." My throat, dry from coughing, croaks my downhearted appreciation.

Placing the tray on the bedside table, the nurse bustles around the room, repositioning my bed further upright before settling a small table with short legs over my lap.

"Do you think you can manage on your own, or would you like some help?" The nurse lifts the tray of food and places it before me on the squat table.

The scent of weak coffee and a hard-boiled egg waft toward me, turning my stomach sour. "I can manage." I offer a slight smile as the nurse gives my shoulder a reassuring pat.

"I'll be back in a bit to collect the tray. Be sure to eat up before it gets cold." Without another word, she is moving toward the door and onto her next task of the morning.

"Ah, wait." My age-spotted forearm lifts from the bed and hovers warily in the air.

"Yes, Miss Bruno. Is there something else?" The nurse turns toward me and strides with the ease of youthful exuberance to my bedside.

"I was wondering if you know when June—" I catch myself and dip my chin in as demure an expression as I am able. "My niece will be back?"

The nurse's hand immediately warms my shoulder. "I imagine she won't arrive until after ten o'clock."

"Ten o'clock? What time is it now?" I feel a ripple of agitation speed toward my chest, settling there with a tightness.

The nurse checks a watch pinned to her immaculate white uniform. "Just past seven now."

"Oh." I have nothing else to offer in my disappointment.

"Hospital visiting hours begin at ten." The nurse gives my shoulder another squeeze. "Don't you worry. I am sure your niece will be here as soon as she can. It is nice to have someone who cares for you so much. You are lucky, Miss Bruno. Not everyone has someone special to visit them."

The nurse inclines her head toward my breakfast tray. "I imagine a hearty meal will help keep your energy up, for when your niece arrives, I mean."

My gaze falls to the tray in front of me as the nurse tells me she will return to collect the empty tray, her voice emphasizing the word empty.

A fresh wave of disappointment consumes me. How am I supposed to tell June anything if she isn't here to listen to what I have to say? This is all my fault. I've wasted too much time being untrusting.

I've spent the better part of twenty-nine years alone. I should be used to it by now. Yet, here I find myself, wishing for the door to open and for June to be on the other side of it. I expect, in the end, we all want kinship in our lives.

I never got the chance to start a family of my own. For years, I traded that dream for one that included George and a life of living on the outskirts of the law. There were good times. Of course there were.

The trundle of a cart moving through the hospital corridor beyond my slightly ajar door takes me back in an instant to the bustle of hushed voices as they bounced between two brick buildings in the narrow alley hiding a secret entrance to the hottest speakeasy in the French Quarter.

Thirty-Six

AUGUST 1925

NEW ORLEANS

MEG

GEORGE'S HAND GRIPS MINE AS HE PULLS ME further into the pitch blackness. Our host for the evening, the man we purchased a truckload of Caribbean rum from, leads the way. With business behind us and a shipment of the good stuff ready to be loaded into our false wood truck in the morning, George is living up to his word and is taking me dancing in the famed city.

Nevada is no stranger to dodging Prohibition laws, George had told me once, but New Orleans is another world altogether. You haven't heard jazz until you've heard it in the French Quarter, he said to me this morning as we lay snuggled together in bed, our lovemaking infused with reckless abandon given our time in this glittering city.

His words tickled a side of me I seldom had the opportunity to indulge. I lived a fairly secluded life on the vineyard before arriving in Elko, and since becoming part of George's crew three years ago, I learned early on that the job of a bootlegger is not a life consisting of one long shindig. To be a successful bootlegger, one must put aside fun and focus on the business.

Despite serving drinks at The Bluff for two and a half years, when The Absinthe House Bar door opens with a secret knock and a password whispered by our host, my whole body tingles with anticipation. The music reverberates within me as George slides my coat from my shoulders and hands it to the burly man standing behind the desk of the coat check closet.

The beaded skirt of my knee length dress vibrates of its own accord against my sheer, silk-stockinged legs, eliciting flashes of sparkle in the chandelier lit room. We move toward a plush corner booth in the shadows of the smokey room. The paisley papered walls add to the intimacy of the space while a well-stocked bar draws my eyes up to take in its ceiling-high shelves.

With three of The Absinthe's signature Sazerac cocktails before us on the small round table, George clinks my glass and watches keenly as I take my first sip. Notes of licorice and spice dance across my tongue, drawing a wide and appreciative smile to my lips. After sharing a drink with us, our host bids us farewell, saying he'll see us in the morning to load up the truck with the rum we've purchased from him.

I meet George's gaze, eager to move my feet to the soulful, edgy beat of the band. Taking my hand to help me from the booth, his hand deftly moves low to the back of my waist as he guides us onto the dance floor. Any inhibition I might cling to is smoothed away in an instant with the rhythm and the liquor coursing through my veins. A bubble of excitement erupts from my lips in a whoop as the band strikes up a familiar tune. My heels kick and I spin, sending my skirt high enough to bare the bottom edge of the garter belt doing its best to hold my stockings in place.

The night goes by in a blink, and as we down our last cocktail, I am certain a raid itself wouldn't put a damper on this night.

Thirty-Seven

AUGUST 1955

ELKO, NEVADA

MEG

"How are we doing with breakfast?" The friendly nurse's chipper voice startles me from my reverie.

I force what I hope is a pleasant smile and offer a polite reply. "Still working on it."

A quick nod of her head and she's out the door again, calling over her shoulder, "I'll check back with you then."

Yes, we had our share of laughs and even a few celebrations.

I pick up the fork resting beside the plate. Looking back, though, I am more than aware that my life had far less meaning than I thought it did at the time. Sometimes I wonder if after disappointing my parents so deeply, I came to believe I didn't deserve an important life, one with family and a husband to call my own. I didn't deserve to be happy.

George certainly echoed the sentiment when news of the baby, the miracle gift we'd conceived during our trip to New Orleans, was lost. Sadly, as I was reeling from a loss I was

208 "

certain I would never recover from, his relief was written across his face.

I suspect I might have known what I was giving up, but now with less life ahead of me, I am certain I made the wrong choice. Staying with George became a habit, and like most bad habits, he was hard to break. I loved him once. But, staying with him while knowing in my heart of hearts there was no future for us, was a decision I made because I had nowhere else to go, and I found myself too afraid to venture off on my own.

At forty-seven years old, I had never been on my own. I had no friends outside of George's crew. My home was directly tied to an illegal business he helped me set up, and my days were spent among those immersed in a life of crime. I may not have been a thug or a gangster, but I certainly knew a few.

My fall from grace was all-consuming the day my father caught me with the sacramental wine. I went from being a well-educated, respected woman to becoming a misfit of the law and, most regrettably, someone else's patsy. Seeing no other option before me, I remained, letting George, the boys, and even my brother dictate what I did and where I went.

All my days, I allowed my life to be decided by others. When my first love died tragically at such a young age, I stayed at home on the vineyard because my father had told me it was the place for me to be while I grieved. I was comforted at the time as he held my hand and promised to take care of me in my time of need and uncertainty.

Over the years, I have wondered if what made sense at the young age of twenty-two didn't hold water at the ripe age of forty-three. Perhaps it's why when my brother came to me, I was easily convinced when he insisted I help with bootlegging the wine. I loved my life on the vineyard, but it came with the strings of my living as my parents' child and not as the independent adult I quietly wished to be.

I went from my father's household rules to following Matteo's insistence on working for him, to being immersed in George's full steam ahead, illegal lifestyle, never stopping to ask myself what I might want. The blame is not only theirs. I had a hand in not choosing a life for myself. I realize now, not making a choice is the same thing as making a choice. In the end, it's a passive decision rather than an active one.

A chill runs through me, sending my body into a spasm of shudders. The table and tray resting over top of my legs vibrates with the shiver, spilling coffee onto the paper placemat on top of the tray. I take a small bite of toast then egg, washing it down with a sip of lukewarm coffee to show the nurse I've attempted to eat something.

Glancing at the half-closed door again, a strangled sigh escapes my closed lips. I miss the girl's company. No, it's more than that. Tears gather in my eyes. I miss having someone special in my life. Someone who knows me and cares for me. Someone who can and wants to advocate for my wellbeing. Someone like June.

All these years, since my time in jail, I've tried to convince myself that I was being a strong, independent woman in an age where women aren't always recognized for such things. But, from my current vantage point, I see now that I have incorrectly assumed that being independent also meant being alone in the world. I've realized far too late—this is not the case.

I want someone else to know the real me. Fully and

completely. Inside and out. I want to confide in June and can only hope she will accept me once the truth has been spoken. There is nothing, save for June's companionship, left for me to lose.

I may have been slow to grasp the importance of being among others, but now I know for sure. I no longer wish to be alone. And I have no desire to die alone. I take another sip of coffee, the lukewarm beverage soothing my throat.

No. I want to be surrounded by family.

Thirty-Eight

JUNE

HAVING SLEPT LATE AFTER MY MIDDLE OF THE night wake up, my hastily eaten breakfast of bacon and eggs from the cafe next to the motel isn't sitting well as I pull into the hospital parking lot. Putting the car in park, I pause, unmoving, while I gather my thoughts along with my nerve. In the light of day, I am no more comfortable with the task at hand. Pressing Meg, I am certain, from all she has told me, is in her best interest. However, I feel little comfort in having to do so, knowing what I now know about her diagnosis.

I feel my bottom lip slip between my teeth, and I check the time on my watch. Visiting hours began fifteen minutes ago, and I wonder if Meg might worry about me if I don't show up soon. Given her state of ill health, I hesitate to imagine her thinking much about me, but is it a risk I'm willing to take? Putting an old woman through any amount of stress or worry, just so I can sit in the parking lot and ruminate. I think not.

Though not facing the music is appealing in this moment, I am well aware my options are limited if we are to locate the sense of peace the woman is seeking. Meg needs to face her past, and I need to bear witness to it. This is what matters most. I take the key from the ignition and tuck it into my bag. With a hand on the door handle, I take a long steadying inhale and push open the door.

I climb out of the station wagon and head toward the hospital's main entrance, slinging my bag over one arm as I move. Lifting my chin, I am mimicking a confident stride, hoping to feel the sensation ripple through me.

I smile politely at a couple sitting on a bench near the front entrance and overhear a snippet of their conversation. "The doctor said we have to keep her calm. Her getting upset is exasperating the situation. We need to avoid any type of confrontation right now."

My foot catches on the curb, causing me to stumble forward, as the man's words strike at the heart of me. For the first time it occurs to me that my questions, my pushing Meg to tell her story, may be harmful to her now. My heart sinks at the realization. What if my presence in her life is at fault for Meg's current hospital stay?

I make it through the main doors but hesitate, unable to move toward Meg's room. The monochromatic white hospital color scheme blurs before me, forcing me to lean against a wall to steady myself.

"I'm fine," I say to no one in particular, shaking my head. "June, you can do this."

Taking a few steps forward, my legs reconsider my mind's certainty with a wobble that unnerves me. I keep walking, determined to help Meg come to terms with her story. The guilt over causing the woman, who is literally fighting for her life, harm, mixes with utter disappointment at the possibility of not seeing my role in Meg's life through to the end. The only thing I can agree to in this moment, is to determine how she feels about where we left off yesterday.

A light rap on the closed door gains me entry. Meg is resting, just as she was yesterday, her torso elevated in the narrow hospital bed. I force a cheerfulness I don't feel into my voice. "Good morning, Meg. I hope you had a restful night."

I keep talking, certain if I lose momentum, I will lose my resolve too. "I see you've had some breakfast. That's good."

Her mouth opens as if to speak, but I push forward, not allowing her the chance.

Stepping closer to the bed, I paste a smile in place. The cautioning words from the man on the bench outside the hospital doors play on repeat in my mind. I look at Meg and see a woman, beaten down by life and illness. I hesitate. I don't want to be the one responsible for causing her more pain, even if the end result is that which she desires.

I change tactics, with fear instead of thoughtful consideration, leading my decisions. I blurt out what is sure to put a stop to all the immediate suffering. "I've come to tell you we should end our interview. I don't imagine my pestering questions are doing much good at allowing you to rest and recover."

"End?" Meg's eyes grow wide in question.

"Yes, it's just that—well, I think it would be best if I come back to town when you're feeling better."

My gaze falls to the floor, shame over my inability to stand strong in the face of a difficult situation, forcing my chin to my chest. "I'm sorry if my presence has caused you to fall ill. I never intended to put your health at risk with my many questions."

"You aren't to blame for my illness. Or this hospital stay, for that matter." Meg's voice is hoarse as she tries to push the half-eaten tray of breakfast farther down the bed.

My fingers fiddle with the strap of my bag, twisting and turning the leather handle between both hands before I drop it onto the empty chair. "Well, even so. I imagine you will recover much faster if I am out from underfoot." I busy myself by removing the breakfast tray to the small table beside Meg's bed, doing my best to avoid her imploring eyes.

"You can't leave, June. Not yet." Meg's voice crackles as she pleads with me, rooting me to the spot. "I have so much to tell you."

I sneak a glance from beneath my lowered lashes, and Meg stares back at me. She isn't angry or even perplexed. In fact, there is little emotion left in her words and her expression reads as calm, and she appears more certain of herself than she has since our paths crossed only three days ago. She does not appear to be a woman experiencing any kind of stress.

My head tilts back as I examine her more closely, a question percolating in the corner of my mind. Perhaps my knee-jerk reaction to me causing Meg harm is off base. Could I have been right all along? Does Meg truly want to confide in me the secrets of her past?

I'm letting the awareness of Meg's cancer diagnosis cloud my thinking. I can feel it in my gut. It would be foolish not to test her resilience on the matter. Testing the waters, I grab my bag from the chair and grip its handle tight in my hand, determined to assess our path forward. I ignore the pull of the connection I feel brewing within me to this woman, steadfast in my desire to ensure I am doing right by her.

"I really must go—" She doesn't let me finish my sentence.

"June, the thing is..." Meg's eyes pool with emotion. "I am dying and you are the only one who can grant me my last wish."

Thirty-Nine

MEG

Are my words enough? I search the girl's face for a hint of confirmation. I am desperate for her to stay. My mind races through the scenarios elicited by the thought of being left on my own. None of them are pleasant. I've finally let someone in, and the thought of June's presence in my life slipping through my fingers feels like a dagger to my heart.

I grip the bed's side rail and try to pull myself up, frantic to convince her to stay. "June, please."

The girl steps toward me, placing a warm hand on top of mine. "Meg, I am so sorry."

Unsure if she is sorry that I am dying or rather she is apologizing for leaving my side regardless of my short time left on earth, I feel as though I am facing down the barrel of a gun.

Anguish over my current situation yanks fresh tears to the forefront. "I don't want to be alone anymore."

Suppressed emotion gathers within me like an out-of-control freight train laden with decades of dissatisfaction and fear. "I've disappointed many people in my life." The tears roll down my cheeks with reckless abandon, but I force my eyes to lock on June's. "But I've disappointed myself the most. I let others decide my fate for so long that I forgot to be an active participant in my own life. I fear I am too late to fix that now."

June's hand squeezes mine. "Don't say that."

The girl's voice coos, and my emotions settle a fraction at her words. I wonder if she will still feel the same about me once I've told her everything there is to tell. Haunted by the thought of disappointing June, I let my tears fall until no more come. All the while, the girl stands beside my bed, holding my hand in a show of comfort and solidarity.

There is little else to do. The only way I can be sure the girl will stay at my side is to be honest with her. I shift my legs, attempting to find a sliver of comfort, if only in the physical form.

June releases my hand to fluff a pillow behind my head before helping me to recline into the pillow's support. Considering where to begin, I remind myself that I must trust the girl and her ability to forgive me for the past. It's the only way forward. First, I must break her heart before there is any hope I can help mend it.

She watches me with patient intensity as my gaze darts about the room. I clear the hoarseness from my throat and begin with what I should have said the first day I met her. "I've made many mistakes through the years." My shoulders shrug in defeat. "I followed the lead of others and in doing so, I had little influence over my life. I came to depend on the wrong people for safety, security, even for love. Leaving my parents' vineyard the way I did, I promised myself I would never let someone I cared for down like that ever again. I let the fear of doing so hold me prisoner in relationships that did not serve me well."

The room goes quiet between us as I think back to that day in the vineyard. The day my entire life changed because my brother had a job for me. "He said he couldn't do it without me and I doubted my self worth enough to believe him. I was a broken woman when I arrived in Elko."

I meet June's gaze, determined to reach her heart. "I have no intention of leaving this world as one."

"George?" June's voice is pensive, and I imagine her piecing together what I've told her so far with my latest confession.

"Yes, he was certainly a big part of it."

"I thought so." The corner of June's lip quirks up. "He didn't sound like the kind of man one could rely on, even if he loved you."

"You understand then. How important it is to never let yourself down, even if it seems easier in the moment to go with the flow of other's expectations." I aim an inquiring eyebrow in the girl's direction. "Of course, you already know the ending when it comes to George. Believe me, it's easier to see the train wreck for what it was while looking backward."

"I'm sure." A small sigh whispers from her mouth. "I am familiar with the concept of trying to keep my head above water in a sea of opinions. My father has strong views on my future." June's lips twist and I sense her unwillingness to speak ill of the man who she clearly loves despite the frustration that comes with the relationship. "My mother assures me he does so out of love, but honestly, I don't think he can help himself. Assumes he knows best and all that."

"He may very well know best." June's head snaps up, a flash of annoyance narrowing her eyes in my direction. I pat her hand, an attempt at quelling her fury. "But that doesn't mean you should stop thinking for yourself. You, as they say, are the captain of your own ship, June Monroe. You must steer it how you see fit. All I'm saying is, take your father's concerns into consideration before writing them off entirely, but still make up your own mind in the end."

A firm nod from the girl shows me she embraces the sentiment while her words tell me she remains vulnerable on the topic. "Must it always be through rough waters, though?"

"It seems so." I let the words sit between us a moment, hesitating at the mere thought of it. "But if I had the chance to hear my father's advice again, I would give him my undivided attention and hang on every word. That, I am certain of."

June slips her hand out of mine as the friendly nurse reappears at my bedside.

"I see you've got company." Her eyes take in the barely touched breakfast tray on the bedside table. "Still not much of an appetite, Miss Bruno."

I shake my head.

"Well, you can try again with lunch." Grabbing the empty cup, she examines its contents. "At least you are drinking. I'll just top this up. Back in a jiffy."

We sit in silence as the nurse bustles back and forth. A lightning strike of panic courses through me as the thought that this untimely interruption may be enough cause for June to reconsider staying with me. I can't let her leave now. Not when we are finally getting to know one another as women should. We are making headway and finding common ground. The more we share about our commonalities, the better equipped we are to support one another.

"There we go." The nurse chirps as she returns with a full glass of water. "Let's take a sip now, shall we?" Lifting the cup toward me, I dip my chin and sip. The cool water soothes my throat like a Nevada rain storm after a summer's drought.

"Thank you." I squeak the words as she places the cup on the table beside my bed and lifts the now cold breakfast tray.

"I'll let you two visit, then." With a warm smile directed in June's direction, the nurse vacates my room with a steady tempo of the squish of her white-soled lace-ups against the stark white hospital floor.

The door to my room shushes closed as the words I need to say bubble up to the surface, bringing with them a heated flush to my skin.

"George wasn't the only one I shouldn't have trusted." I blurt the words out in a rush, desperate to convince June to stay.

Forty

JUNE

MY DESIRE TO LET MEG BE SMOLDERS AND SPITS like a campfire being doused with water before being extinguished entirely. She has, in her own words, assured me this is our path forward. There is more to Meg and her story, and I'm still trying to figure out how it all fits together. I pull a chair closer to the bed and take a seat. Sneaking a glance at my watch, I realize it has taken us the full amount of time I originally allotted for the interview to arrive at this point. When I arrived in Elko exactly forty-eight hours ago, I was eager for a quick meeting. I thought I'd gather my notes and be on my way with everything I needed for a front-page article.

Sitting here now as Meg's life experience is about to be revealed, I can't pinpoint why, but I'm certain I was meant to get involved in the woman's life, no matter how long or short it is. Listen to my instincts, that's what I've got to do, I tell myself before lifting my eyes to meet Meg's.

"Thank you for staying." Meg's expression reveals a sheepish side to her and my heart swells knowing, even if our conversation doesn't end up as a story worthy of the front page of *The Carson City News*, I've made the right decision. Some decisions are best made in the moment, with the heart leading the charge.

I cross one leg over the other and settle into the chair. "Seems like we have more in common than we may have originally thought."

"We do," Meg agrees, as a soft smile lights up her face.

"Do you want to tell me who else you shouldn't have trusted?" I scrutinize Meg, almost expecting her to duck and cover like she has had a tendency to do since I met her, but she surprises me with a subtle nod of her head.

"I suppose it is time."

"I suppose it is." Resting a bent elbow on top of my knee, I lean forward and give my full attention to Meg.

"My brother, Matteo." Meg's eyes dart up to check my reaction before finding comfort in the view of her hands clasped on top of her lap. "He became someone I couldn't trust."

"When he asked you to help him by bootlegging your father's wine?"

"Should have been a warning sign for me." Meg's shoulders lift then fall with what I assume is the weight of her past mistakes. "I knew better. Even in that moment, I could feel the wrongdoing while I was agreeing to help him with his plan."

"He was your older brother. I can see how you might have felt obliged to him."

"I did."

I bite my lower lip in hesitation, unsure of these

uncharted waters of conversation between us. "Do you ever ask yourself where your obligation to Matteo ended and his taking advantage of you began?"

A knowing smile slides into place on Meg's face. "I had a feeling you read more into his true nature than I divulged. How did you do it? I hardly gave you a lick of information."

I return Meg's smile with one of my own. "Call it reporter's instinct."

Meg's laugh startles me at first with its hoarseness, but within seconds we are both chuckling. We have been side-stepping and calculating our responses to one another for the past three days. The lightness that comes with knowing we can be honest with one another is an immense relief, and one I am grateful for.

"Actually, I pieced it together." I sit back in the chair and lift one finger up. "Bootlegging your father's wine was your brother's idea." I lift another finger. "He refused to allow you contact with his family when you lived in the same town, presumably working for his advantage in the black market." I raise a third finger. "Matteo inherited the family vineyard when your parents passed, and I assume he continued to profit from it on both sides of the law for several years more."

"That about sums it up, yes." Meg's agreement of my assessment brings a furrow to her brow.

"There is something else, though. Something you haven't said." I press the topic, hoping she won't shut me down again.

"There are many things I haven't told you yet," Meg demurs.

"I am sure you're right. What I really want to know is,

did your brother have something to do with your going to jail?"

The room falls silent, save for Meg's fiddling with the sheet that lies across her lap.

I swallow hard while resisting the urge to say more. I don't shift in my seat or take my gaze off of Meg. The longer I wait the more I am convinced of the answer. Why is the truth such a difficult thing to give voice to? Do we assume the mere words will hurt us so?

I let the minutes tick by until Meg's hand settles and she retreats into herself, once again finding comfort in staring at her hands folded in her lap.

I clear my throat so as not to startle her. "Earlier you spoke about not disappointing yourself. This is your chance to decide your life's trajectory." I give her a moment to consider my words.

"I know this is difficult, Meg, but you are at a crossroads now. This is one of those moments that you will either be proud of or regret for eternity."

Meg's head bobs, but the woman gives no indication of saying more.

"Not just for you, but for me as well."

My words draw her out. She is listening.

Tucking my hesitation away, I brace myself, knowing I must ask a difficult question. "I assume your prognosis." The words hitch in my throat. "It isn't good, is it?"

"No. I'm afraid it's not good news." Meg's frown is pulled tight. "I have lung cancer."

Moments pass like hours as reality presses down on us. "They say I've got a month. Maybe a little more."

Moisture gathers in my eyes at the same time a tear rolls

down Meg's cheek. Our shared grief at the short time frame cementing our bond further.

~

SEVERAL MINUTES PASS BETWEEN US. I clear my throat, breaking the hush. "Alright then, it seems we have work to do." I push aside the emotions that are threatening to spill over. I am no good to the woman if I dissolve into a puddle of tears. Our timeline has, without a doubt, been shortened and I have no intention of letting Meg down.

Meg meets my eyes, and I can feel several questions pushing forward, vying to be asked at once.

"You agreed to speak with me because you had something you wanted to say. I understand your hesitation to dig up the past but, if we're going to tell your story and set the record straight, then we need to get to work."

I lean forward in my chair, imploring her with my eagerness to get started. "This is your chance to have your say, Meg. You told me you didn't wish to go out as an outcast. The only way you don't, is if you speak the truth about what really happened in 1926."

My legs are antsy and ready to pace. I heed their warning, but don't give in entirely. Instead, I stand, scraping the chair's legs against the stark white hospital flooring. I grasp Meg's hand in my own. "I won't let you down, Meg. We don't even have to publish the article if you don't want to. But I know in my heart that you need to be freed from this self-imposed prison of regret."

Meg squeezes my hand in hers. "What about your career

as a renowned reporter? Nellie Bly, wasn't that who you aspired to be?"

Hearing the teasing tone in her voice, I feel the heat of a blush, and I know I am about to turn pink from my head to my toes as the slightest hint of embarrassment causes me to do without fail.

"You'd be willing to give that up—for me?"

"Some things are more important. I'm here for you as long as you want me to be."

Meg's posture straightens as much as is possible in her semi-reclined state. "Good. How do you feel about a memoir?"

"Memoir?" As the word leaves my lips, I can see the story unfold before me. The beginning, the middle, and the end. All of it the way Meg wanted to tell me from the start. This was never about a newspaper article. This was always about her life.

Forty-One

MEG

THE GIRL'S FULL BODY ROSINESS TAKES SEVERAL minutes to subside. I stifle the chuckle that is keen to escape, and instead focus on her expression as she comprehends the breadth of what I am asking her to do. The resemblance is subtle and though she looks nothing like my more prominent olive-skinned Italian heritage, beneath the surface, I can pick out traits of a familial lineage from the northern region of my mother's homeland.

I watch her with bated breath as she continues to process. Understanding she is likely unaware of her roots, I assume she is also unfamiliar with the depth of character that comes with our Italian heritage. Throughout history, family has been at the center of our world. Mix the importance of our family ties with the pride we maintain in being persons of solid character and my reasons for doing what I've done become even more clear.

I see it more than I ever have since meeting her. How my

past and her future are intertwined. I was right to agree to meet with June. I just didn't realize how right it was at the time.

"Memoir?" June asks again.

"Yes, I am ready to tell you everything. Even if you are the only one who hears it, I no longer wish to keep the secrets of my past." I swallow hard, trying to push down the emotion rising within my chest. "I no longer wish to be viewed as an outcast throughout history—"

I take as deep a breath as my lungs will allow and prepare to admit for the first time, the true reason I am ready to speak about my past. "I no longer want to be misunderstood by my family. I am ready to set the record straight, and I want you to be the one to do it."

"So, even before I arrived. I was never meant to write a newspaper article about the events of the 1926 raid?"

My head shakes with slow, purposeful movements. "I never meant to mislead you. In all honesty, I've been grappling with my decision all this time." I force myself not to look away. "When you telephoned and asked for an interview, it was as if an opportunity opened up for us. It just took me some time to get used to the idea."

"For us?" The girl's eyebrows lift in question and the junction of past and present, that we've been moving toward, is finally upon us. This is where our lives intersect.

"I can explain." I incline my head toward the floor. "Though I suspect you'll want your notebook for this."

June squeezes my hand reassuringly before letting it go. Taking a seat in the chair beside my hospital bed, she reaches into her bag and pulls out her notebook and pencil.

Forty-Two

MARCH 1926
ELKO, NEVADA

MEG

"THE TRUTH SHALL SET YOU FREE, MARIAGRAZIA." The priest's words play on repeat through my mind as a hive of reporters, lawmen, and Elko's curious swarm in circles inches away. Behind me, their voices buzz throughout the courtroom in a quest to secure new facts, gossip, or lies. Beyond the rail that separates me from them, I can feel their accusatory whispers and the heat of their stares as they bore into the back of my head, while we wait for the judge to don his robe and take his seat.

I don't mind the delay. In all honesty, there is little else for me to do but wait. I've become a patient woman over the past two months, waiting on this continuance or that objection and more than once on the judge himself, as he seems unable to keep a schedule of any sort given his frequent tardiness.

The first time the judge arrived late to court, where I was concerned, I had to smother a snicker behind a palm when he appeared with rosy cheeks and a slightly disheveled fluster about him. Among Elko's bootleg circuit, we are well-informed of which city officials frequent specific underground establishments. Scanning the courtroom, I draw an imaginary line between the prosecutor, the bailiff, and even the court reporter. All of them are in good company when it comes to the judge's afternoon imbibing, since each one of their names is on a list at one Elko speakeasy or another.

I think about my own business and its select clientele. The Bluff has successfully remained under the radar of city officials, a circumstance I imagine I owe to my brother and his connections in the police department. A small sigh slips past my closed lips. The liquor has likely been collected by George and the boys by now. Leaving it lying around is simply asking for more trouble if it was found. I have no desire to have further charges levied against me, given the two months I've already spent behind bars.

The shudder running the length of my spine is an automatic reaction to my damp, and far from hospitable, jail cell. In response, I direct my thoughts elsewhere. At least the courtroom has a window to the cloudless blue sky beyond. A much cheerier view indeed. The room is also a touch warmer than the block wall of my secluded little cell, not to mention the musty scent that somehow permeates concrete is, thankfully, absent in the courtroom.

Jail is, for the most part, a tranquil place to wait, save for the less than comfortable aspects of the accommodations. Since I am the sole female resident at the county jail, I have been given my own cell several corridors away from the men who have found themselves in the similar predicament of being incarcerated. I am visited three times a day by a rotation of a handful of guards delivering a meal, water, and the brief exchange of words.

The few sentences I choose to speak in a day, the pleases and thank yous, reassure me I've not lost, or forgotten how to use, my voice or my manners for that matter. I fear the priest may be correct in his counsel of freedom, but still, I find myself unable, or perhaps unwilling, to speak the truth. For one, I find what I suspect is the truth to be unbearable and thus unspeakable, and second, no matter what may come my way, I am by no means free of guilt. I knowingly disobeyed the law and so I hold my tongue, accepting the punishment as my own.

Out of duty, love, obligation, or, as I suspect the priest thinks, pure pigheaded stubbornness, my silence has done little to shield me from the charges they eventually laid against me.

I stifle the cough that is desperate to rattle out of me. The damp, dank quarters of my jail cell have made my lungs weak, or so the doctor who visited last week seemed to think. I dislike dwelling on things I cannot control and instead turn my attention to maintaining my posture. The hard-backed, wood chair, not designed for a woman's frame, is too deep for me to rest against, so it is up to me to hold my head high while remaining stiff as a board while I wait to learn my fate.

After the feds raided George's warehouse on January 12th, and found me standing among heaps of contraband liquor, they took me into custody. Despite having no proof of any wrongdoing on my part other than where I was discovered, the barrels of my father's bootlegged wine literally betraying me that fateful day, I was detained for weeks before they finally charged me with selling alcohol to minors.

The whole thing is a sham, and everyone in the courtroom knows it. Connecting the warehouse raid to the scant number of liquor sales at the local high school is a stretch, even for Prohibition agents eager to celebrate another win against the big bad lawbreakers of Elko.

My lawyer has tried to reason with me, knowing there must be other factors at play. I'm certain the man is going bald solely due to my persistence to remain mute. Matteo knew what he was doing when he asked me to help him bootleg our father's wine back in 1922. He had a lifetime of assuredness that I would keep his secrets, no matter what was at stake. Family protects one another, after all.

Forty-Three

AUGUST 1955
ELKO, NEVADA

JUNE

I WILL MYSELF TO REMAIN STILL. MY LEG WANTS TO bounce. The anticipation of finally learning all Meg has to say is enough to make sitting patiently an arduous chore. My pencil is ready to fly but Meg has drifted off once more, staring at the blank wall, its white on white color scheme blending with the rest of the room in nothing more than a blur, I presume.

Though I'd love nothing more than to barrel ahead with the questions that are cued up and waiting to fire, Meg's diagnosis has proven to dampen my zealous nature. I heed all that I've learned when it comes to Meg and decide it's best to give her time to be alone with her thoughts. She is trying to come to terms with a significant amount of emotional tug-of-war and however I can support her in doing that is what I must do now.

My thoughts return to Meg's request of me. I am surprised to know she is asking me to write her memoir. Me, a proper writer of someone's life story. I've never considered tackling such an immense responsibility, always setting my sights on a career as a newspaper reporter. That is, I admit to myself, feeling the silliness of my rationale along with the heat of a blush as it spreads from beneath my collar, how Nellie Bly got her start. I suppose there is more than one way to achieve a goal. Nellie Bly wrote a book.

Meg no longer wishes to be misunderstood by her family. The words turn over on repeat in my head. Perhaps it's the woman's failing health that has her confused. I was certain she said she had no family left. Or did she? I tap the eraser end of my pencil against my cheek as I think back to an earlier conversation.

Maybe I misunderstood and her angst comes from the fact that she is no longer in contact with any of her family members. That would explain things. I scratch a reminder into my notebook. I will ask someone at the paper to do some digging for me, see if we can locate a family member or two for Meg. Even if she decides not to share her story with them, I am certain they will want to know about her current condition and reconnect while time allows.

Thinking about her family, I'm confident she told me the truth about her parents passing back in the early twenties. Given Meg's age, they wouldn't be likely to be alive now. But what of her brother? Could Matteo still be alive?

My knee vibrates, bouncing up and down like a rubber ball on a sidewalk. If Matteo is alive, that would explain Meg's reluctance to share the events of the 1926 raid. The pieces are falling into place in my mind. No wonder she's been so cagey. If Matteo is alive, he isn't likely to want to have his past exposed. I am understanding Meg in a new light. If Matteo was really as manipulative as I imagine him to be, then she may have concrete reasons to be unsettled over the thought of a reunion with her brother.

And what did she mean by an opportunity opening up for us? Is she referring to the memoir or something else? I am quickly compiling a list of unknowns and find myself back in the position of having more questions than I do answers once more. This all must come together, somehow. I am eager to have it all make sense and with the whirring of my mind refusing to slow, the silence of the subdued hospital room closes in on me, as my patience to hear what Meg has to say wears increasingly thin.

Forty-Four

MEG

I'M NOT SURE HOW LONG I'VE BEEN LOST IN thought. My wandering mind is becoming a habit, and one I am not comfortable with in the presence of others. The girl is waiting for me, her notebook open on her lap, ready to begin. I get my footing as an image of my brother rumbles through my mind. "You were right about Matteo. I believe he betrayed me in the end."

June sits taller in her chair. I almost expect to hear the words, *I was right,* fly from her lips but she holds her tongue and waits for me to continue.

"I've wondered about it plenty over the years, but in the end, I didn't find the strength to accept the truth of the situation, not fully anyway. That ends today."

I pull the stiff hospital sheet upward, feeling the need to shield my insecurities with the only thing available to me. "You see, it couldn't have only been my brother who did wrong by me. George and Matteo had to both have been involved in order to pull off such a scheme."

My fingers grip the edge of the sheet, turning my knuckles white with what little strength is left in my body. My head shakes back and forth of its own volition. My disagreement with the situation makes itself known in every fiber of my being. Whether it is the acceptance of the truth or my inability to see things for what they were all these years, I am uncertain.

"Even in jail, when I found myself near death's door with weakened lungs, I wasn't able to come to terms with the truth. Anytime I came close, I pulled back and accepted my punishment. I deserved such a punishment, after all." My shoulders deflate in agreement with my confession. "I lied and stole from my parents. Those ill-fated actions were only the beginning of my many misdeeds."

I catch the sight of June leaning forward in concern from the corner of my eye. The tears gathering there make it difficult to see the girl completely, but I sense her compassion.

A bark of a disgruntled laugh lurches out of me. "Even when it was clear pneumonia had me in its grips and my survival was uncertain. While the priest prayed over me, I refused to speak of my inkling that Matteo and George had arranged for my demise in order to save themselves." A long exhale slides from my lips, draining my entire body with it. "That was why I was released early from jail, you see."

I lock eyes with June, her pencil hovering above the notepad resting on top of her knees. "I wasn't expected to survive the damp conditions with pneumonia. Antibiotics weren't as prevalent as they are today so the judge was persuaded by both his conscience and the priest to set me free with time served. It wasn't likely, in my sickly condition, that I'd take up with more illegal business practices."

June's head bobs in understanding before returning her attention to scribbling with haste in her notebook.

"You see, I've had plenty of years to consider the facts, and there was no way the feds were aware of the liquor I sold to the high school students. Not on their own, anyway. The kids turned me in, it's true. But they certainly weren't inclined to confess and put themselves in that kind of hot water over liberties taken several months before if they hadn't been coerced to do so. The high school liquor sales would never have seen the light of day, not unless someone else gave me up first. I imagine all it would take is a whisper to a parent of one of those students. That could have easily started the ball rolling."

My eyes flick up to June. "Besides the students themselves, the only ones who knew were those in George's crew. None of them would put a foot out of line without George's approval, so even if he didn't spill the beans personally, he most certainly knew the person who did. I suspect he directed them to leak the information to the right people."

The girl's brow knits together as her nose scrunches up in question. "How did Matteo know then? I didn't realize he was in George's crew."

"He wasn't. At least I didn't know he was, not until it was too late, that is. I had always known Matteo to be careful not to get his hands dirty. Not to put himself too close to the fire, so to speak." My head drops into my hands at the reminder of my lack of awareness and all it cost me in the end.

"When I first arrived in Elko, Matteo told me George and he were merely acquaintances. I mean, I figured George bought Matteo's black market wine from my father's vineyard, but so did several other men who were distributing Prohibition liquor to speakeasies and pharmacies throughout the country. It didn't seem out of the ordinary for them to have that kind of business-like arrangement."

June's head bobs as she makes notes.

"After meeting me at the bus station, I seldom saw my brother. If we came across one another in town, we pretended to be strangers, to protect one another and our mutually illegal behavior. I never saw Matteo and George together, though my father's wine still managed to make its way into George's warehouse. George didn't speak of Matteo after that day at the bus station, and what's more is nobody in George's crew ever mentioned Matteo either. I knew well enough not to ask questions I didn't want an answer to, but I didn't suspect anything was out of sorts since my brother never came up in conversation. Until the day he did."

I gather my courage, hoping it will be enough to carry me through as the words hang in the air between my lips and June's notebook.

"It wasn't until George and I came to blows about our future one night that George let it slip. All those years I was close to George at work and in other ways, yet I was completely in the dark when it came to how deeply connected my brother and George were."

I feel my lips twist and taste the remnants of this morning's coffee, bitter and stale on my tongue. "The night I pressed George about marrying me, I was in a right state. I was overcome with grief and more distraught than I'd ever been about anything else in my life. I hadn't slept in days and was inconsolable, having lost our unborn child a few evenings before."

June smothers a gasp with a fist, her hand pressing in hard enough to form a pucker of lines around her mouth.

My head shakes at the thought of that night. "I pushed him to his breaking point and beyond in that moment. I thought he loved me. He told me he did. In fairness, he might have loved me in the only way he knew how. I should have known better than to trust the word of a man who lies for a living."

A disgruntled chortle emerges from my chest, followed closely by a weighted sigh. "I was four months pregnant when everything went wrong. Though we hadn't planned for a baby, I quickly came around to embracing the idea. I hoped a change of lifestyle and maybe even location would allow us to have a normal life."

I tuck my embarrassment along with my chin at such fanciful notions. "I spent months lost in a daydream of a cozy little home in a state with four seasons. Vermont appealed to me back then, far enough away from Nevada's blazing sun and the life of a bootlegger. Given its charm, the quiet of a sleepy little town seemed like the perfect place to raise our family."

Twisting the sheets between my hands, the memory sears my heart like a hot poker, reminding me of the pain that spasmed through me that dreadful night. I try to clear the constriction from my voice with a raspy cough. "Where I was devastated about our loss, George was relieved. I couldn't wrap my head around it. The man I loved was actually lightened by the loss that was breaking me in two."

A ragged exhale shudders from within me, threatening

to spur another coughing fit, but I do everything I can to halt the cough in place, determined to tell the rest of the story. "When George was unable to calm me down, he blurted out in frustration that there was no situation under the sun where he would marry me. The words stung, without a doubt, but it was what he said next that turned everything I knew to be true upside down. He said he couldn't marry the boss's sister."

June sits up straight in the hard-backed chair. "What?"

"It's true. Until then, I had assumed George was the head of the bootleg operation. Turns out, it was Matteo all along."

June is speechless, but her shocked expression says all it needs to.

"What's even more stunning is while Matteo was neck deep in a full-scale illegal Prohibition operation, he was rising through the ranks as an Elko city police officer. You see, what my brother held over George and every other man under his employ was his position within the police force. He had access to both the legal and illegal sides of Prohibition. Just think of the power he held in his own two hands."

A whoosh of air escapes with the words I've held onto for far too long. The secret I've told no one until now. "So, yes. To answer your question from before. Yes, I am certain my brother and George had everything to do with the charges laid against me and the subsequent time I spent in jail. I simply couldn't bring myself to believe it before now." A sad smile toys with my lips. "They hung me out to dry to save their own hides. My biggest downfall was my affection for each of them. Both men knew I would remain silent out of loyalty and love."

"I can't believe your own brother sold you out like that." June is out of her chair in an instant, notebook in one hand and pencil gripped tight in a white-knuckled fist of the other. "You must have been furious."

"I imagine you can see now why it took me ages to come to terms with the notion. Part of me still wants to believe they weren't involved in sending me to jail, but..."

"But nothing, Meg. You were innocent and served significant time for them." The girl is in a heated state now, making short loops back and forth across the width of the room. "I knew yours was a story of righting a wrong. I could feel it in the pit of my stomach."

June takes another lap, tossing her notebook and pencil to the chair as she passes. "I'm so angry I could scream. Who needs enemies when you have family like Matteo? What a lowlife."

"Don't forget." I caution her anger fueled enthusiasm. "I wasn't entirely innocent, June. I was, in fact, guilty of many things." I suppress a smile at her eager response to come to my aid. "You must know, I've come to terms with my punishment, my role in things, but I appreciate the support. Truly, I do."

"I'm not sure how you're so calm right now. You were right. This story is much bigger than a newspaper article." She pauses her stride and meets my eyes with fire in hers.

I could be tempted to leave things as they are. A little voice inside my head whispers the possibility. Depart this world knowing that June knows the truth of my past and still supports me, believing in the unjust aspects of my life. But, then again, I argue back, is it still a lie if only part of the truth has been revealed?

I take a deep breath to steady my nerves, determined not to give up on what I've set out to do. Too many times, I've not been courageous in the moment I needed to be. That approach certainly hasn't served me well all these years. "June, there is something else I have to tell you."

Forty-Five

JUNE

THERE'S MORE? THE QUESTION IS ON THE TIP OF my tongue when the door to Meg's hospital room whooshes open with the gust of a breeze, halting our conversation abruptly.

"Ah, Miss Bruno." The same nurse who poked her head in earlier enters the room with a cheeriness that seems out of place for the emotionally fraught conversation between Meg and me. I swear I can feel the air crinkle like a thunder bolt rumbling ahead of a strike of lightning as her presence shifts the energy in the room.

Both our heads swivel in the nurse's direction.

"It's time for your vitals and lunch." The nurse issues a pointed look at me as she steadies a fresh tray on Meg's side table. Though a smile pulls her lips tight, her demeanor makes it clear she means business. Directing her comment to me, she says, "If you can give us a few minutes. There is a vending machine down the hall and to the right if you'd like to get yourself a refreshment."

With a reluctant nod, I comply. Grabbing my bag, I move toward the door. "I'll be back in ten minutes." I hope to reassure Meg with my statement, but I direct my intention to return soon in the nurse's direction and raise an eyebrow for emphasis. Pushing down the fury over Matteo that has yet to settle, I do my best not to unleash it on the friendly nurse and instead plead my case. "Please don't sedate her. We want to spend our time together." A final glance in Meg's direction, and I am out the door.

The bright overhead lights make the trek down the long white corridor feel ominous and dizzying. I am still reeling from the confirmation that Matteo and George are the reason she spent several months in the Elko County jail. My heart has difficulty imagining a scenario where a family member or even a friend would betray me in such a way. How they used her compassion and care for them against her raises the hairs on the back of my neck.

My father's face emerges in my mind's eye. Even he, who I frequently butt heads with, would never do such a thing. Saving himself by putting me in danger would never cross his mind. That I am certain of. He is an outstanding man. A strong and determined one, yes, but also loving, kind and generous. I am not sure Meg could say that about George or even Matteo.

The hair on the back of my neck refuses to stand down, sending my thoughts to wind back even further, to a time when another man's words elicited a similar reaction in me. I was nine years old in the summer of 1941 when my grandfather took me to the Carson City fairgrounds to see the traveling circus that was in town for the week. The war in

Europe was filling the newspapers, but the United States had yet to get involved that summer.

My memories, like those of most Americans, I imagine, are book-ended by a timeline of before the war and after. The messy bit in the middle doing little to spur happy tidings when so many lives were being lost overseas. I remember the day clearly. We shared candied apples and tossed rings to win prizes. Spending time with my grandfather was a welcomed treat, allowing my mother an entire day to spend with her own mother in the garden that stocked our cupboards right through to winter.

We were waiting our turn in line at the merry-go-round when a man I'd never seen before sidled up beside my grandfather. The man wore a dark hat not suited to the warmth of the day, with its front edge pulled low, casting a shadow over his face. He leaned in and whispered words fast enough to send spittle from his lips. My grandfather's face turned to stone as his hand, gripping mine, clenched tighter, causing me to shriek in response.

He apologized to me with kind eyes before directing his attention to the man. In a whispered warning, he told the man he didn't owe him a dime, saying, "you got what you earned more than ten years ago. Our business is finished." When the man tried again, my grandfather's free hand grabbed him by the collar so fast, I jumped in response. My grandfather's voice was low and threatening, lifting the hairs on the back of my neck. When he finally shoved the man away and we moved ahead in line, he smiled at me, telling me everything was alright before asking if I'd like a cotton candy once our turn on the merry-go-round had finished.

I remember being too frightened to ask him who the man was or why he was bothering us. I spent the entire time seated upon the frolicking horse of the ride searching the crowd for a glimpse of the man. I never told my mother or anyone, for that matter, as my grandfather had told me it was our secret. He explained on our way home how his job meant he had dealt with some unsavory characters through the years and he wouldn't want to worry my grandmother by bringing up such mentions. We didn't have many outings after the circus, and a few years later he passed unexpectedly in his sleep. Speaking of such things seemed disrespectful to his memory, and since such an incident only happened the once, I brushed it off and took him at his word, aware, even as a young girl, that some things are better left unsaid.

I give my head a shake, wondering where the random memory of my grandfather that I haven't thought of in years popped up from.

My father's face reappears as I turn the corner toward a waiting room I have yet to explore. His smile and boisterous laugh remind me of the good times shared between us. The way he likes to dance with my mother in the living room when her favorite song comes on the radio. His bad jokes and inability to deliver a punchline lift the corners of my mouth.

I MEANDER down the hospital corridor as a new understanding percolates. My view of my father softens with each step, and the compelling awareness that I have been judging him with a harshness he may not deserve. The shame of how I've behaved toward my father creeps in. Like Meg said, he could very well be right about a lot of things. In all honesty, I haven't given him much of a chance to explain himself in recent months. Instead, I've acted like a four-year-old who didn't get the piece of stick candy.

My mother's prodding echoes in my periphery, reminding me of a time not that long ago when my father and I were inseparable. For most of my life, he included me in everything. Whether he was fishing at his favorite watering hole, teaching me to dance by standing on the tops of his feet as we moved around the living room, or showing me how to drive and change the oil in the car, he did his best in raising me. He showed me I could take care of myself.

Somewhere along the way, I stepped out of his shadow, as I expect most children do when they're on the verge of growing up, and our once harmonious existence crumbled under the weight of our changed relationship. The more I tried to make my way in the world, the more challenging our interactions became. This, I realize now, is how I've gotten it into my head that he doesn't trust me to make the right decisions.

I reach the vending machine and plunk in a nickel before selecting a soda I have no interest in drinking. The machine hums, then clicks as it releases a bottle into my hand. When I think back, my heart pried open with the perspective of Meg's experience, I am able to see how much he supported me. My father not only encouraged me toward further education, he also helped me gain employment at *The Carson City News*.

Even when he resisted the idea of his little girl becoming a reporter, he helped pave my way. I never thought to ask why he didn't approve of my career choice. I must have assumed he thought I wasn't capable enough to take on the demanding role. Like Meg, I am not without fault. I've crafted my own stories of my father's thoughts and opinions of me. Stories that, I realize now, have been oversimplified to serve my own purpose.

I traveled all the way to Elko, intending to give a woman I didn't know, a woman convicted of a crime, no less, the benefit of doubt. My knees buckle at the thought of it. Pivoting, I rest my back against the wall and let my chin drop to my chest in shame. I didn't even give my own father the same courtesy, and we live in the same house.

"You can do better, June Monroe." I say the words out loud, determination to correct the trajectory of my relationship with my father gathering steam. Meg may not have the opportunity to repair the damage caused between her and her parents, but the woman's greatest regret is sure to help me make certain that I won't allow my pride and my desire for independence to ruin one of the most important relationships in my life.

I can be both June the reporter, and also June the beloved daughter. It will take communication and effort and require me to forgive and be forgiven. All relationships require that sort of care, and I am keenly aware I haven't been properly tending the relationship with my father. As my mother always says, two things can be true at the same time.

I inhale a deep cleansing breath, resolved to set things right and ensure my family knows our relationship is one that I cherish. I will work to keep our connection with one another a priority. Family is a cornerstone of life. A smile inches my cheeks upward. My mother taught me that.

My thoughts return to Meg and her lack of family relations. It can't be easy, facing death with no one to walk alongside you. A glimmer of hope ignites within me. I wonder if the one more thing she has to tell me is that

Matteo is indeed alive. Perhaps she wants to reunite with him. Forgive and forget, and all that.

Though I can't say I would rush to do so knowing what I know now. Then again, I haven't had thirty years to contemplate the situation. If Meg wishes to reconnect with her brother, I will do everything I can to help her do so.

I check my watch and note that fifteen minutes have passed. Spurred by the desire to return home and make amends with my family, I walk with hurried steps down the hall. My hope is, above all else, the nurse has not given Meg another sedative.

Forty-Six

MEG

THE NURSE REMOVES THE BLOOD PRESSURE CUFF from my arm and smiles. It is the *poor dear* expression I read in her eyes that reminds me—my time is short.

"I was going to tell your visitor, your niece, is it? To come back tomorrow. The doctor doesn't want you to wear yourself out." Her nasally voice borders on reprimanding, and I can hear the hint of a tsk threaded through her words. "Honestly, I expected your numbers to be through the roof, Miss Bruno. But since everything looks stable, I will allow your niece to stay until dinner is served."

"Thank you." A disquiet I hadn't known I was holding onto due to the lack of control I am currently faced with releases, and with it, an exhale. "Thank you very much."

The nurse tidies her instruments away before making a few notes on the chart that hangs at the end of my bed. She moves to stand beside me and cocks her head to one side. "Until dinner is served, Miss Bruno, and not a moment longer." Her scolding tone is undermined by the nurse's lopsided grin and her reassuring hand on my arm.

"I understand." The care of this stranger catches me off guard, warming my heart. But her kindness isn't enough to thaw all the years of solitude and desperation.

No. Only the kindness of a family can do that.

"Meg?" The girl is standing at the door, asking permission to enter with pleading eyes.

"You two have a few hours before visiting time is over. Miss Bruno needs her rest." The nurse turns on her heel and pulls the door all the way open for June to pass through. "I'll make sure your dinner is the last one delivered." She winks at me before disappearing into what I imagine is the bustle of a hospital corridor.

June steps further into the room. "What was that about?" She asks, gesturing over her shoulder.

"Just a little kindness for an old woman."

"Oh." June sits in the chair positioned at the side of my bed. "That's nice."

I sense the girl is waiting for me to continue what I started before we were interrupted. I swallow the lump in my throat and clasp my hands together tightly in my lap, willing them to act like a grounding rod for the charged words I must share with June.

"As you are aware, my given name is Mariagrazia Brunelli. My family originated in Italy and we came to the United States for new opportunities when I was a small child, barely able to walk two steps on my own. My father worked day and night for years on the small plot of land he could afford, selling his grapes to other winemakers until he had accumulated enough resources to make and sell his own wine. My parents were equally proud to be Italian and

American. In the Napa Valley, our heritage and customs weren't much of an issue since the area had many foreigners living among the hills and vineyards."

June remains still but her body, angled toward me, suggests her patience may expire if I don't get on with it.

"Growing up, my brother, Matteo, and I were desperate to become more American. We wanted hamburgers and French fries instead of risotto and tiramisu. We were also desperate to shorten or change our very Italian names to something a school mate could wrap their tongues around."

I shift my position, seeking comfort where there is none.

"When it was just the two of us, Matteo would call me Maria and I would call him Matt." I smile at the memory. "We even had a pact, going so far as to poke our hands with the sharp end of one of our father's grape knives to draw blood before squishing our hands together, bonded by our secret, always and forever."

Understanding dawns on June. "That's how it started. How he knew you would keep his secret." June's voice trails off. "Always and forever."

Emotion rises in my throat, making my delivery of what I must say that much more difficult. "Secrets are seldom good. Not when they are fresh and exciting, but especially not when they are tired and worn out and in need of being revealed."

"I suppose this is when you tell me you've got a secret to tell me?" June leans in and places a hand over top of mine folded in my lap. "It's okay, Meg. I think I know what your secret is."

Startled, I search the girl's eyes for understanding. She is taking the news exceptionally well if she truly knows what I am about to divulge.

"Matteo is alive, and you want me to help you locate him." June appears pleased as punch as she makes the declaration.

"Wh—what? Where did you get that idea?" The questions stutter forward as I grapple with the knowledge that I not only have to disrupt June's world with the truth, but I also have to crush the notions of what she assumed was a clever theory.

"I—well, I guess I thought. You seemed keen. Like you wanted to make amends with your family. I figured Matteo was the most likely candidate given that you already told me of your parents' passing."

"No, that's not it. Matteo is very much deceased and I know exactly where he is. Six feet under in the Carson City cemetery." I almost shout the words, unable to gain control over my fraught emotions.

"Oh." June's hand slips from mine as the girl leans back in the chair, her mind whirring in what I assume is an attempt to comprehend what I've said.

Unable to do anything but plow forward, I tune out the girl's misguided assumptions and hope with all my might that somehow, some way, June will find it in her heart to forgive me.

"Much to my parents' dismay, my brother aspired to be a police officer instead of a grape grower. He had little interest in making wine and even less inclination for the grapes themselves. He had scoped out the scene in Elko and thought he'd do well there, except for his name, that is. When he met with the sergeant in charge, it was suggested to him he change his name with the intention to tone down the derogatory comments he might experience if he flaunted his Italian roots."

I sneak a nervous glance in June's direction. Sucking in a quick breath, I exhale and let the truth slip out with it.

"A week before he applied for a position at the Elko police station, Matteo Brunelli became Matt Johnson." I steal another sideways glance in June's direction, trying to gauge her reaction. "Shortly after my sentencing in March 1926, he became the Chief of Police in Elko. He remained in that role until he retired to Carson City with his wife several years later."

June's mouth falls open, and her face grows pale. It takes her a few moments to register the information. A crease forms between her eyebrows, and I imagine a multitude of questions stampede through her head. "That can't be. My mother's father was named Matt Johnson, and he was a Police Chief in Elko years ago. He retired in 1933 just after I was born and they moved to Carson City to be close to my mother and me, their only grandchild."

The girl's voice transforms from solid and certain to wavering and stilted. Tears spring to her eyes, placed there by an anguished heart as understanding invades her awareness. "You mean..."

"Yes, it's true. My brother was your grandfather." I've only known the girl for three days and yet I feel her pain in this moment as keenly as my own. Moisture builds and gathers in my eyes before the tears flow like a river down my cheeks.

"I don't understand." June's eyes, laced with fury, flash in my direction. "You must be mistaken. My grandfather was a kind man who loved his family. I don't understand."

I have nothing to argue against the girl's view of Matteo. To her, I have no doubt the master of secrets and double lives was indeed an upstanding individual. "I am sure he was."

"But what you're saying is…"

"I realize this is a lot to take in, June." My throat tightens and the desire for another sip of water presses in on me.

"My grandfather is your brother?" The girl's anguished bewilderment is stretching her face in all sorts of directions. "But he was an only child. He told me so himself."

June's declaration stings. The brother I gave up my life and eventually my freedom for wrote me out of his life when it became convenient for him to do so. The fresh awareness of the depth of his cold-heartedness chills me to the bone. Out of instinct, I reach for the covers and wrap them as far up my body as they will go.

"You're saying he lied to us?" June's eyes gather with tears. "About everything."

"I'm afraid so." As soon as I say them, I want to reel the words back. "Not everything. He was a police officer too. That part is true."

"But he was—a criminal. If what you are saying is true, my grandfather lied to everyone for decades, even going so far as to use his position as an officer of the law to break the same laws he was supposed to be upholding."

I can't tell if she is about to lay blame at my feet or embrace me in a hug. *The truth shall set you free,* the priest told me all those years ago. I summon the courage, determined to let the truth speak for itself. "Yes. Matteo was good at that."

"Arghhh." June stands abruptly, knocking the chair back as she moves, sending it skidding with a screech across the floor. "I don't know what to say."

Pacing the room, the girl runs a frantic hand through her

hair and then stops. "So many lies. I don't know what to think." Dropping her head into her hands, mere seconds pass before sobs vibrate through her body.

I know, intimately, the immense grief that comes with such understanding and nothing I can say in this moment will bring the girl peace. The cost of voicing the truth comes with the hefty tax of shattering another's serenity. This is what I feared most, causing harm where there was none before.

Through muffled words, I hear, "Oh my heavens, I'm going to have to tell my mother. This is going to devastate her."

Forcing myself to remain silent, I do all I can to give the girl the space she needs to confront the news I've placed in her lap. I am at a loss of what to do next and decide to let June steer our course. I am certain she hasn't made all the connections yet. That will take months, if not years, to sort through what she believed was true, compared with the new reality before her. But we are family, June and I. Though she never knew I existed, here I sit. The family outcast. Her great aunt. And also, the Bootleg Queen my brother never spoke of.

"I can't believe this. He just lied. My grandfather spent his entire adult life lying—to everyone." Her emotions are running rampant on full display and hard to miss from across the room where she is ranting as a fresh wave of realization hits her.

She pivots on one heel and moves back in my direction, the agitation in her voice at full throttle. "Right up until the day he was laid to rest, he was heralded as an outstanding citizen. Do you know how much brass came to his funeral? It was all pomp and circumstance. I mean, there was a color guard and an American flag draped over his casket, for goodness' sake."

This is excruciating for June, as I imagine it will be for her mother. I remind myself that I did not put either of them in this position. I may have delivered the news, but it was Matteo who set the lies in motion all those years ago with little regard for anyone else in his life. I am left to wonder if my brother ever loved anyone, save for himself, that is.

The days ahead are likely to be challenging and far from simple, but I have to admit, the priest was right. The truth did set me free, but it isn't the sort of freedom I was expecting. Instead, it is a sense of peace I feel, knowing I've finally, through gritted teeth and tear-bleary eyes, told my side of the story.

Forty-Seven

JUNE

AN HOUR PASSES WITH SPEED AS I PACE AND FUME and question every memory I can pull forward in this moment. "He was a fraud. Plain and simple." A hiccough follows my tear-infused, and incredibly disappointing words, as the stories Meg has shared with me about her brother filter through my mind's eye with a new lens.

Meg sniffles, drawing my attention her way. The connections are coming fast and furious now, like a row of magnets lined up close enough to one another to snap together with an earsplitting crack.

"This is why you've been following my career. The newspaper clippings in your scrapbook. You knew who I was all along." I take a step closer to the bed, resisting the urge to close the gap between us, not trusting myself to remain calm. "And you didn't tell me."

"I've been trying to tell you. That's all I've been trying to do since the moment you knocked on my door. June, please.

You have to understand." The woman's pleading does little to edge out the fresh sense of wariness rising within me.

"I have to understand?" My lack of a calm demeanor over the truth placed before me leads my voice to lift a turbulent octave higher. "I can't believe you're asking me to understand. Right now, I'm not sure I comprehend any of this."

"I didn't tell you straight away because I had no way of knowing what you knew of me and, honestly, I've been struggling to understand the same thing you are trying to comprehend right now. Lies and falsehoods are all that have cloaked me for ages. I couldn't know for sure. I didn't know what he might have told you. How you and your mother might have felt about me. I never intended to hurt you. I—I just couldn't bring myself to risk being rejected again. I'm not sure I could survive another rejection." Meg's voice falters, breaking both in sound and delivery, before continuing. "I see now. Matteo's secret went with him all the way to the grave." Another tear slides down Meg's cheek. In my current state of distrust, I question whether her emotions are due to all she's lost or her awareness of how difficult the truth will be on me and my family.

She must know what is reeling through my mind. Her eyes seek mine out, desperation shining in them. "I went to prison for him, June. I hope that tells you as much about me as it does about my brother."

A ragged sigh slips through my lips as I concede her point. If Meg has taught me anything in the past three days, it is that she is a woman who takes responsibility for her actions, values the importance of family, and above all else, the woman is loyal to a fault. I drag the chair back to Meg's bedside and collapse into it. "You're right. Actions always trump words."

"I would have come looking for you sooner, but part of me believed I didn't deserve a family." Meg's shoulders lift a fraction, her familiarity with untrustworthy people having made its mark on her. "When you telephoned the first time, I almost fell right out of my chair."

The image of Meg's shock lifts the corners of my mouth. "I imagine it came as a surprise. A telephone call from your long lost—"

"Niece." Meg fills in the blank as the reality of our family connection clicks into place in my mind.

"You're my aunt." It seems obvious now, but given the all-consuming news about my grandfather, my brain hasn't yet worked out the rest of the details.

"Your great aunt, actually." Meg's expression brightens as she nods her head. "We are family, June."

"And you." The original reason for my trip to Elko, the newspaper article I was supposed to write, pops into my awareness, making me queasy once more. "You want me to write a memoir about you? About my grandfather and our family?"

"I believe you can, yes. I've read every article you've written for *The Carson City News* and you really are very good." Meg lifts her hand to me, and I take it. "But only if you want to and most certainly only if your mother agrees. I have no desire to cause this family any more pain."

She gives my hand a reassuring squeeze. "Telling the story, the truth of my life. That was all I needed to do. The rest is up to you, June. You can do with it what you wish."

Despite her age, the cancer, and the challenges her life

has presented her, Meg shines with more vitality than I ever imagined she had in her.

I contemplate her encouraging words, balancing my desire to write something important, something that will make a difference, against my fears of how what I write might be perceived by others. My parents may resist the idea, or maybe they won't. Perhaps once they've heard the complete story, they will see the significance of righting this particular wrong. I know one thing for certain, this decision is not mine alone and deciding whether to publish Meg's story will take time and open dialogue with my parents. Regardless of the end result, her story is a place where we can begin again, as a family.

Our hands remain locked together, and I lean in, lifting my gaze to meet hers. "I will write your memoir, Aunt Meg. I can't promise it will be published, but together, even if it is solely for us alone, we can set the record straight. For the sake of our family."

Fresh tears glisten in Meg's eyes, and I see for the first time the family connection we have in common. I stifle a chuckle, knowing our shared stubborn streak is likely responsible for bringing me to Elko in the first place and is the same trait that kept me here, even when I wanted to leave.

Forty-Eight

FEBRUARY 1957

ELKO, NEVADA

MEG

"It's here!" June's voice lifts with excitement. She is out the door, closing it tight behind her in a rush. The screen door thwaps quietly against its frame as I imagine the girl dashing down the porch steps to the mailbox at the end of the driveway. The new door, one of the many household repairs I owe to June's father, Albert, does a fine job of blocking out the crisp whip of wind that often accompanies a February afternoon in Elko.

June has been waiting for the postman all morning, seldom venturing far from the new narrow window that came with the updated front door. A chuckle emerges as I consider the poor postman when he catches sight of the girl running toward him at full speed.

Much has changed in my life in the past eighteen months. My life, for one, has far outlived the doctor's expectations. I know my time on earth remains as short as my breaths are shallow, but I am overcome with gratitude for the family that has steadied me and given me a reason to live as well as a reason to hope.

Meeting my niece and her husband for the first time felt like coming home. Our initial meeting at the hospital remained awkward for less than thirty minutes as I saw in Helen, just as I had in June, a distinct Brunelli family resemblance. We grieved over the years lost to lies and secrets, but soon found ourselves immersed in filling in the blanks. Helen's tears fell fast and hard when it came to stories of her father, and though I can't take her pain away, I am grateful to be here to wipe her tears and hold her hand as she wades through the grief of learning who he was.

The more time we spend together, the more familial traits jump out at me. Seeing June or her mother's full body blush continues to warm my heart. But it is Helen's facial expressions and mannerisms that almost stopped my heart the first time I recognized why she seemed so familiar. If Helen resembles anyone in the Brunelli family, it is my mother. Watching my niece putter about the kitchen or bend to pet the cat is akin to seeing my mother do the same thing all these years later. I am grateful for the time we share with Helen and Albert's weekly visits, as they make the trek to Elko each Friday evening after Albert finishes work for the week. The ease with which we have formed a relationship continues to bring me immense joy. Even Albert and June have mended fences, both of them finding their footing as father and daughter once more. In eighteen months, we have done our darnedest to make up for the more than fifty years lost to us, and for that I am grateful.

The cat is curled and lying at the foot of my new sofa, doing a reasonable job of keeping my feet warm. June dashes through the front door, shaking the cold from her uncloaked torso. Marching toward the sofa, parcel in hand, she gives the cat's head a rub before holding out the package.

"Aren't you going to open it?" Despite the rasp, my voice lifts with teasing cheerfulness.

"Not without you, I won't." June deposits the box in my hands, then heads to the kitchen for a pair of scissors.

The girl's exuberance is on full display as she snips the air playfully with the scissors as she returns to the living room. "Are you ready?"

I hand her the box with a wide grin, stretching my cheeks upward. "Ready."

She makes quick work of the package, slicing the top and sides before placing the scissors on the coffee table. "Here we go." June oozes enthusiasm as she removes some extra paper padding, dropping it to the ground. "It's beautiful."

The box falls to her feet as June lifts the book from within. She places a palm flat on the cover as a muted gush slips through her lips. Turning it over in her hands, she holds it up for me to see. A square black-and-white photograph of me with my back to the camera is nestled at an angle within a peacock-blue cover. The title and subtitle, written in an elegant font, catches my eye.

BARRELS OF BETRAYAL: The Life and Times of Elko's Bootleg Queen as told to June Monroe by Mariagrazia Brunelli.

"You did it, Aunt Meg." Tears pool in June's eyes.

"We did it." I say, lifting a finger to swipe the dampness from my own cheeks.

June runs her fingers over the book's cover, inspecting every inch with pride. I hold my breath until she finds it, my heart skipping a beat when she flips the page and the dedication is before her. The last thing I will ever keep from June is the note I mailed to the publisher, requesting they print my dedication instead of the original agreed upon one.

> *To my fearless June,*
> *May you always find the strength to chase the*
> *light, no matter how dark the shadows*
> *seem.*

~

JUNE

MEG GROWS tired easily these days. I lay an extra blanket across her legs, knowing she'd rather be too warm than the slightest bit cold, and decide to let her sleep. After an emotional few moments as I read and reread her surprise dedication to me, and another hour spent oohing and aahing over the first official copy of our book, I slip into the kitchen to begin dinner preparations.

As I putter about the small room chopping vegetables and simmering broth for soup, I think back to how much my life has changed. I never would have imagined I would live in Elko, let alone with Meg. A year and a half ago, when I first met her, she was a cantankerous old woman, and I was an over-eager reporter looking for a story to make my mark in the world.

Things changed straightaway and dramatically, for all of us, once Meg told me her secret. My parents, upon receiving a tearful telephone call from me, arrived in Elko the next day. Their shock of meeting Meg and learning who she was took a few days and a thousand questions before sinking in. By the end of the week, our little family dynamic had shifted, as if Meg had always been a part of our lives as she and my mother shared family stories, filling in the blanks of what each of them had missed out on.

When the doctor informed us Meg could leave the hospital to spend her last days at home, I didn't hesitate to offer my help, promising the doctor she'd be well cared for. A few days later, I quit my job over a telephone call to Harold at *The Carson City News*, explaining I was going to focus on Meg and the book we were writing together.

Meg lets out a light cough in her sleep. I place the knife on the cutting board and peek around the wall separating the two rooms to check on her, but she hasn't woken. Back in the kitchen, I pull a few carrots from the fridge and think about my life now. When the weather turned cooler, I sensed a shift in Meg. With each passing day, her breathing has become more labored. Wheezing inhalations are staking their claim within her tired lungs. Time is running out.

I consider the moments we've shared. The late-night conversations and the days spent poring over the stories of her past. She's helped me navigate topics ranging from my relationship with my father, to the prospect of love and marriage, to my career path. The relationship with my father is where I feel Meg's guidance the most, since she sat us both down and told us it was her dying wish to see us reconcile our grievances. She spoke frankly of the importance of family, her tears doing just as much as her words when it came to nudging my father and me to talk over the challenges we'd been facing.

In the end, he told me that after years of listening to Harold go on about the horror stories that came with reporting the news, he was scared. The last thing he wanted was to see his baby caught in the crosshairs of something dastardly. He was trying to protect me. He wasn't attempting to snuff out my light so I couldn't shine. With the four of us agreeing to move forward with the publication of Meg's memoir, my father was the most vocal about my involvement in writing it with Meg. The lightness that came with having my father on my side, rooting for me again, made tackling the immense writing project feel exciting, rather than daunting.

Over the past several months, I've learned to appreciate Meg's strength, her tenacity, and also her quick wit. I laugh out loud at her sense of humor and admire her ability to remain patient, especially in the throes of adversity. Above all else, I have come to love my Aunt Meg.

There will never be enough time.

My heart swells with gratitude for the woman who entered my life far too late, but also precisely when I needed her most. She has instilled in me the importance of claiming my life as my own, while respecting those who love me. Because of Meg, I will marry if and when the right person enters my world. I will forgive and ask to be forgiven when I falter. I will love with my whole heart, even when I might get hurt. Most of all, I will tell the stories that need to be told. The ones I am compelled to tell because Meg showed me the importance of lifting my voice to be counted in this world.

I move toward the kitchen table and reread the letter that arrived a few days ago. Without Meg's encouragement, I might have dismissed the idea altogether. Now, though, I see in me what she did back in 1955. Tomorrow I'll write to the publisher and let him know I will gladly accept his offer and write my next book, a story about a woman who, similar to Meg, did what most people wouldn't.

None of us could have imagined Meg would fight back against the cancer and gift us these months together. My grandfather, Matteo, was wrong in so many ways, but he was right about one thing. Meg's love knows no bounds.

Forty-Nine

MEG

I WAKE TO A SILENT HOUSE. JUNE REMAINS ASLEEP in my bedroom, I presume. It's early still, but I can tell by the brightness in the living room, and the hush beyond, that snow is falling outside. There is a chill in the air, so I tuck the quilt a little higher. A ragged breath tells me all I need to know.

I'm seventy-seven years old, and I give more of a damn now than I have in years. These past months have been the greatest gift of my life. I can't say that if I'd known what I was truly missing out on that I'd have reached out to my family sooner, but I am grateful for June and her willingness to embrace all of me. With her by my side, I have relearned how to love and how to be loved.

The cat jumps down from the sofa, stretching his paws in front of him in anticipation as June pads into the room wrapped in a robe. Stooping to scratch his head, she greets him how she has every morning since moving into the house. "Good morning, Kitty. Are you ready for breakfast?"

A light chuckle accompanies my smile. "He's gotten used to having you around. I think he enjoys being spoiled."

"I enjoy spoiling him." June moves to the window by the front door to peer out. "It snowed last night."

"I figured as much, the air feels like snow. Is it deep?" I ask, already knowing the likelihood of my getting up to take in the view of winter is unlikely now.

June adjusts the quilt lying over my legs. "A full blanket of white. Not a speck of desert to be seen. How about you? Are you ready for breakfast, too?"

"I could do with a cup of tea." I wiggle my arm from under the blankets and lift a hand toward her.

June takes my hand in her warm one and gives it a reassuring squeeze. "I made a fresh loaf of bread yesterday. How about a piece of toast?"

Though I won't eat it, the offer warms my heart. "Toast would be lovely."

June turns toward the kitchen.

"Before you go, can you pass me the book?" I want one more look. One more moment to soak in the accomplishment I am most proud of. The book is evidence that I did what I set out to do. I told my side of the story, and no matter how history judges me now, I've made peace with my past.

June passes me the book before bending to plant a light kiss on my forehead. "I really am proud of you, Aunt Meg."

"Proud of *us*, June. Proud of us."

The girl smiles, but sadness waits, hidden beneath her upturned lips. She wipes a tear before it falls and heads to the kitchen to prepare breakfast.

I flip through the pages of our book, reading snippets from this chapter and that. Awareness creeps in slowly as I read, and then I can see the epiphany for what it is. The memories of writing the book with June are stronger than the pain of the past. Time smooths all things if you let it, but in order to truly heal, you need love.

"You've come a long way," I tell myself. "A long way, indeed."

My body is tired now, the wheezing a constant companion. I feel sleep pulling me under and grip our book tighter in my arms, not wanting to drift off. I could beg God for another day, another week, but we both know better. There is never enough time when there are those you love still walking the earth.

~

JUNE

THE AROMA of freshly toasted bread wafts into the air as I spread a dab of butter over its lightly browned surface. A whistling kettle spurs me to remove it from the burner and pour the boiled water into my great grandmother's teapot. The teapot and single teacup were the only items left to Meg after her mother's passing. Like so many other things about Meg, the heirloom makes more sense to me now.

Kitty weaves through my legs in what I assume is a gesture of gratitude for his now consumed bowl of kibble. I settle the tea and toast on the wooden tray, adding the jar of strawberry jam Meg favors.

I lift the tray from the counter, ready to announce breakfast. The distinct thump of a book falling to the floor in the living room stops me in place. The tray hovers a few inches above the counter as I listen, praying and waiting for a murmur of her wheezing breath to pierce the silence. Tears gather and build before rolling down my cheeks. The tray hits the counter with a clatter of dishes bumping against one another, and the loss hits my heart before my mind has time to comprehend.

Meg is gone.

The idea for The Bootlegger's Betrayal was like a dripping faucet. First an article on the women who supported their winemaking husbands before, during, and after prohibition caught my attention and got me thinking about a woman's role during the 13 years the Volstead Act was enforced. Then a conversation with the ladies of our HNS Afterparty group reinforced the idea of representing women of an older generation in fiction. Lastly, like a lightning bolt, on the evening of the publication date for Growing into Greatness, as I lay my head on the pillow, a brand-new voice entered my consciousness. It was Meg and she had a few things to say.

First, Meg gave me the opening line in the novel and it has stayed as such from its initial inception to the final edition you are holding in your hands. Next, she prattled on about this and that and in my sleepy state, I had the glimmer of a thought that I should be writing all of this down. But I was so reluctant to leave the very one-sided conversation that I chose to ignore the insight to write it down. Meg stopped me at this point and said in her to the point, gruff manner, "you should be writing this down." I smiled at her forthright nature and let her continue. After a dialogue of substantial length she finally said, "you can call me Meg."

The next morning when I woke, I went straight to my desk to write down all that had happened the night before. I wrote down the first line and "you can call me Meg" and when I paused to try and remember what else she had told me, her voice came through again, not so much crystal clear but gravely and determined for sure. Her epic words of wisdom to me... "I told you, you should have written it down."

And that is how I met Meg. Our relationship continued on for weeks before I finally put the idea into motion. This provided me with ample opportunity to get to know her character more deeply. I learned what she was afraid of and what she was desperate to achieve. I learned of her regrets and her sense of humor. I learned that even a woman, tough as nails and a force to be reckoned with, has a softer side and a desire to be known for who she truly was.

The setting of Nevada is not a likely one for a vineyard novel. At least that is what I thought in the beginning. I pushed aside the persistent idea of locating the story in Nevada for many months before I stumbled across the life of Stella Belluomini. In the end, Nevada was exactly the place the story had to be set and I learned once more to trust my initial periphery thoughts and treat them as the gifts they are.

The Bootlegger's Betrayal was inspired by Stella Belluomini's arrest and subsequent jail time, however the fictional story deviated from actual events. For example, Stella was indeed involved in the one of the largest wine raids in Elko in January of 1926. Eight people were arrested, including

Stella, and all of them were charged with selling liquor to minors, while over 820 gallons of wine was dumped into the Humboldt river. Stella was charged with eleven counts of selling liquor to minors while the other seven men were charged with one and four counts each.

Stella operated a speakeasy for some time and there was a shady individual named George mentioned throughout my research. I fictionalized their relationship when I learned that Stella had married, divorced, then married again the same man, with the kicker being that the judge that sentenced her was the same judge to finalize her divorce. In reality, Stella only lived into her forties and not well into her seventies like fictional Meg did.

When I began researching Stella I had a heck of a time trying to find any information. This was due to a continual and plentiful mis-spelling of her last name. The court records, newspaper reports, and more all had different spellings of Belluomini. It was my friend Erin Davies, who finally located a photograph of Stella's tombstone that confirmed the spelling of Stella's last name. With that information in hand, I was able to dive further into the details with Elko archivists and researchers.

The Carson City Newspaper that June works for is a fictional publication but Benny's coffee shop was real and appeared in postcards from the 1950s in images showing it attached to Jay's motel in Elko, Nevada.

During my research I discovered that the Catholic Church's consumption of sacramental wine was limited to the clergy during Prohibition. In fact, parishioners did not imbibe in communion wine until the 1960s so understanding how much sacramental wine was flowing and not required for religious purposes makes the bootlegging of wine that much more plausible. In 1922, when the sacramental wine permit came into existence there were 2,139,000 gallons of wine sold in the United States. By 1924, just two years later, wine sales for sacramental purposes rose to 2,944,700 gallons.

Finally, I may get some push back when it comes to Meg's ability to own and operate a business of any kind in 1926. Her speakeasy front of a perfumery was actually possible due to the Femme Sole Laws of the time. This law specified that unmarried women could purchase and operate businesses without the need of a man's authority. Well before the Married Woman's Property Act, the Femme Sole Law allowed freedoms to never married women that were not afforded to the likes of married, divorced, or widowed women. I love it when history and fiction meet to the benefit of a story.

Acknowledgments

Writing a novel is not for the faint of heart so those that boldly step into the ring alongside an author are to be commended for their support, sacrifice, and contribution to the end product. I am indebted to many and my life is richer because of each of you. From the bottom of my heart, thank you!

Erin Davies, thank you for tenaciously seeking the truth, without it I'd have lost my anchor. To the HNS Afterparty zoom group, thank you for your continual support, insight, and humor-filled conversations. Together we grow, grieve, love, laugh, and learn how to properly slice an onion.

To the women of The Eleventh Chapter, I am honored to be among you. Fierce, loyal, supportive, intelligent, funny, and compassionate. Your talent as writers shine through the best parts of each one of you and I am so grateful to have a backstage pass to watch you soar. HOWARD!

To my beta readers, Kate Thompson, Kelsey Gietl, and Diana Brandmeyer, thank you for taking this journey with me. Thank you for laughing and learning with me and thank you for always having the story's best interest at heart. I'll never get tired of hearing your opinions.

Thank you to my VA, Brianne Matheny for keeping me sane by taking care of all the things I have little patience for and also, for making me laugh!

Thank you to my rockstar team of advance readers. I love sharing my stories with you and I am forever grateful for your enthusiasm, kind words, and constructive feedback.

Thank you to my editors Robinette Waterson and Jamie McGillen. I would be lost within the pages without you. Thank you for your insight, timeline checking, fact checking, grammar checking, typo checking, and overall support and enthusiasm for the story. I am immensely grateful to have you in my world.

As always, I am in love with the cover created by the talented Ana Grigoriu-Voicu. You continue to inspire me with your designs and are an absolute joy to work with.

To librarians everywhere, thank you for loving books, supporting authors, and embracing the challenge of hunting down tidbits of research.

Of special note, thank you to archivist Toni Mendive and archives assistant, Ella B. Trujillo of Northeastern Nevada Museum, Jessica Cole, reference librarian at the Elko Library, and Esther Rigby of the Elko District Court, all of whom provided detailed reference material with regards to the case of Stella Belluomini for whom this fictional story was inspired.

Thank you to my family and friends who continue to be excited by each novel I write and willingly let me ramble about unfinished stories until they come to fruition.

A huge thank you goes out to my husband who rerouted his travel plans by thousands of miles to visit Elko, Nevada on my behalf in search of research for this story. Sometimes you just need to see a place to really understand it. This time, I saw it through my husband's eyes and the contacts he made along the way. It takes a village.

And, thank you for choosing to spend your time reading *The Bootlegger's Betrayal*. I hope the story made you laugh, cry, and explore your own thoughts on family and the secrets they keep. If you enjoyed this novel, I'd love for you to leave a review at your favorite online bookstore or reading platform.

A writer from a young age, Tanya E Williams loves to help a reader get lost in another time, another place through the magic of books. History continues to inspire her stories and her insightful view into the human condition deepens her character's experiences and propels them on their journey. Ms. Williams' favorite tales, speak to the reader's heart, making them smile, laugh, cry, and think.

The Smith Family Trilogy

Becoming Mrs. Smith

Stealing Mr. Smith

A Man Called Smith

The Hotel Hamilton Series

Welcome to the Hamilton

Meet Me at the Clock

Cocktails Before Midnight

A Vintage Vineyard Novel

Growing into Greatness

Stand Alone Titles

All That Was